Unbar the Barred -Previously Ranch-Down

Darling Ranch - Prequel book 1
JP Sayle

Contents

Check This Out First

Unbar the Barred

Was formally Ranch-Down in Knotting Hearts Anthology

Prequel to Darling Ranch Series

It is based in the Divergent Omegaverse Universe

Unbar the Barred

Sex.

No expectations, no dates, no romance, and definitely no emotional entanglements.

Trey lives by these rules, has done for years—until Cassidy changes everything. Only problem, Cassidy is living by the old rules.

One night shifts the balance once more, but can an old wolf learn new tricks for his young, pregnant chick?

Chapter One

Cassidy

His heat was over, or damn near it, and still he craved Trey. His toys were no substitute for the bar owner, who occasionally fucked him in the restroom out the back of his bar, Ranch-Down. Their no-strings agreement was okay, sort of, if Cassidy discounted the part of him that wanted to cuddle after sex. Was it too much to ask for more than a slap to his ass before Trey withdrew, zipped up, and exited the stall to wash his hands and clean off Cassidy's scent?

He tsked at his own neediness when he was a willing participant in what Trey had been clear about from the beginning.

Sex.

That was it.

No expectations.

No dates.

No romance.

Sex. The sex part was what he needed right now. Whatever else was in his thoughts got shoved aside because it would lead to nothing but heartbreak. He followed the need of his rock hard cock, which was demanding something he couldn't achieve alone. Not until the worst of his heat was over.

One glance at his wristwatch and he calculated he had enough time to wash the stink of his heat off him, dress and be at the back of the bar right around closing.

Ethan, the manager of Darling Ranch, wasn't expecting him back to work until the day after next, so it wouldn't matter if he had a late one. His girls would get well taken care of by Sunny, one of the other ranch-hands who didn't mind the chicken stink. His excitement grew at the fact that, for a little while, he was free.

In the shower, he reached for the body wash Trey liked and washed the dried slick from his legs and ass. He had left his toys in the bathroom sink to wash later. His ass clenched as he slid his fingers around his well-used hole, feeling how easily the muscle relaxed, the sensitive skin encouraging him to sink in three fingers, deep. He released a guttural groan, and finger fucked his ass under the steamy water, biting his lip to keep the noise down, knowing how thin the walls were between the tiny workers' cabins sitting on the outskirts of the ranch.

Slick continued to leak from his ass at thoughts of Trey's thick, long cock and how his knot would stretch and burn so good. His toys were never a substitute for the real thing. But needs must and an unexpected pregnancy was not what anyone wanted.

Cassidy took the free hand he had braced on the wall to stroke down his hard shaft. Using the soapiness to glide up and down his sensitive dick, the need drove him to rock back and forth, fucking himself with practiced moves. His eyes darkened with hot thoughts of his last encounter with Trey.

Biting harder on his lip to hold back his whimpers, he tasted blood. He pushed deeper, adding another finger, seeking relief and the same pleasure he got from Trey. When he came there was none of the elation, all he felt was dissatisfaction from his own touch despite a little of the tension easing in his gut. He blew out a breath into the steamy air, working to slow his heart rate down while he finished cleaning himself.

Cassidy attempted to keep his mind empty as he dried and dressed in loose sweats, minus underwear. He grabbed his truck keys off the counter that divided the small space between the kitchen and the living area. All the cabins were the same. A living space, a bedroom big enough for a double bed, with a built-in closet, and a small bathroom with a shower. Rustic, wooden walls and polished floors, it was home, and Cassidy had no complaints when he had a door he could lock and have privacy. Something he'd never experienced as a child.

His sneakers made no sound as he went down the porch steps after locking his door, avoiding the creaky floor-boards. He knew everyone on ranch land, but he was still cautious. He had little, but what he had he wanted to keep because he had worked for it.

It was never truly dark on the ranch with the open sky above, scattered with stars. It was rare for the clouds to obscure them all. Cassidy loved to lie out back on a blanket and stare up at them to remind himself how lucky he was and how much he'd achieved on his own.

The sound of the night birds, animals housed not that far away in barns and out in the pastures and paddocks, carried on the breeze. It was music to him. This was his place. He took a moment to appreciate it before coasting his truck down the hill towards the ranch gates and then starting the engine.

He listened to the radio as he made the familiar trip to town, which only took fifteen minutes. Most of the roads out by the ranch were empty this late. It was only as he drew closer to town that he passed other vehicles.

It took one look at the car lot behind the bar to see he'd miscalculated. He groaned in complaint at seeing some familiar trucks and motorcycles. He debated with himself for all of ten seconds as his truck idled while he decided if he should hang or leave.

Fuck it.

He parked in a spot that the lights didn't reach. Out of the truck, he glanced about, listening to the loud music. It had to be Friday when there was a band playing. One Friday every month, Trey got a band in for the locals.

Time had slipped by Cassidy. He rarely paid any interest in dates or days because they were of little consequence, unless it came to his heat. Then he had to take notice.

The back door opened, and the noise increased, only Cassidy wasn't paying attention to that. His focus was on the huge guy blocking out the light, who happened to be the reason he was here.

Trey was around fifteen years older than Cassidy. Silver streaked his midnight black hair. It hung in a shaggy mess around a rugged face. Dark, leathery skin made his eyes stand out. Green like the sun hitting leaves, so bright they were a reminder of summer when winter came. He was lanky but broad across the back and his chest held solid muscle from carrying beer casks. He filled the plaid shirts he favored, usually paired with low slung Levi's that hugged his ass sublimely. The man was a fucking wet dream, and Cassidy witnessed the pleasure coming into Trey's eyes when he stepped into view.

No matter what the man said, the look he wore now suggested he felt more than a passing fancy for Cassidy. He had his reasons for not wanting more, and they were his own. Cassidy didn't push for more. He had learned over the last two years they'd been doing this—whatever *this* was—that he was an immovable mountain, unless he actively decided differently.

The security lights caught Trey pause, as if considering his next move. The bulging trash bag he held hovered over the pile to his left.

"Well, lookie what we have here?" he drawled. The trash bag got plonked on top of the others. Dusting his hands off, he strolled towards Cassidy. "Been a while, Cass."

Had it? There was no way for Cassidy to say. He wasn't one to measure time when it would appear insulting when he couldn't remember, he'd learned that from others. So he decided to cock out his hip, giving Trey a seductive smile, knowing the game well. Every time he looked into those green eyes, Cassidy lost the ability to think rationally.

The wrinkle of Trey's nose came with a low groan. "You smell…"

Cassidy was on him in seconds. He wasn't for waiting tonight like usual. Didn't want to talk. He needed to feel Trey buried in his ass to quell his desire.

Trey's mouth was as hot and greedy as Cassidy's, while work-roughened palms slipped under his clothing, going for the band of his sweats. Naked underneath, Cassidy whimpered at the thick finger teasing the crease of the top of his buttocks.

"Don't tease me," he pleaded, not wanting the appetizer, just the main course.

Trey's chuckle was so dirty it sent shivers through Cassidy as he ground his aching cock against the thigh pressed between his legs. "Someone is needy tonight."

The rough pad of Trey's finger left a trail of sparks leading deep into Cassidy's channel. It twirled in the stickiness and they both groaned when Trey pushed in hard and fast.

"This what you want, my little chick?" His breathing was harsh against Cassidy's mouth. "You want me to fuck you where anyone can see how desperate and needy you are for my knot?"

"Yes," Cassidy managed to gasp as another finger sank into his ass, going straight to his sweet spot and stroking it until he was close to coming in his sweats.

"That's it..." Trey murmured in between kisses, "ride my fingers, show me how much you want my cock." Trey's tongue fucked into Cassidy's mouth, and he sucked greedily.

Fingers pumping deep in his slick, loose ass, and the dirty talk, had Cassidy humping Trey, whimpering into his greedy mouth.

"Wanna feel my knot so bad, don't you? No one fills you the way I do."

"N-no. No, they don't," Cassidy cried when Trey stopped, waiting for his reply. Cassidy would never reveal that Trey was the only one who had ever touched him. That was his secret.

Trey kissed down his throat, going to the hammering pulse at the base, his teeth grazing the skin, then nipping hard enough that Cassidy's dick oozed along with his ass, soaking his sweats.

"You want it bad enough you'll let me bend you over the hood of your truck and fuck you right here? Right now?" Trey whispered against Cassidy's overheated skin.

Cassidy didn't fucking care, he was burning with desire. "Anything," he cried as four fingers crammed into his ass, making his cock spurt.

Chapter Two

Trey

Each inhale clouded Trey's mind and increased the wild need to do everything that poured out of his mouth. Everything about Cassidy appealed to Trey and right now, he was struggling to stop his wolf sinking his teeth in the heavenly scented flesh and claiming his little chick.

A noise from behind him, followed by a curse and a door slamming, brought him back to his senses and realize that he had planned on knotting Cassidy outside—in public.

"W-what, why you stoppin'?" Cassidy demanded in that sexy, kiss roughened voice that didn't help Trey keep his wits about him.

When they started—whatever this was they had going—Trey had set himself personal boundaries when he realized he couldn't resist the quirky guy that smiled like he was seeing the world anew every damn day. The guy had an innocence about him that, when combined with this sexy, needy side, drew Trey like his whole body became magnetized.

Two years ago, he'd given in to Cassidy's allure, thinking that he would eventually grow bored with Trey and go looking for someone younger, who would give Cassidy what he wanted. To date, that hadn't happened, and Trey didn't dwell on why he could no longer fuck anyone else. Still, he wasn't fool enough to think that it could work long term even when, alone in his enormous bed late at night, he dreamed of such things.

Trey worked long hours that were not conducive to a relationship, as he'd found out. So sex with no-strings was what he'd chosen for the last ten years and, until Cassidy, it had worked.

His belly quivered when Cassidy gave him a pleading look, though he didn't reach out. Didn't straighten his askew clothing or drag up the sweats hanging around his ass. His chick knew to wait, and that added to the appeal.

His wolf listened out and Trey glanced back at the closed door, knowing it would not be long before someone else came looking for him.

"I'm not stopping, just ain't prepared to share the view of your ass with my staff," Trey rasped harshly, noticing the blush that graced Cassity's cheeks, unsure if it was pleasure that Trey didn't want anyone to see but him, or embarrassment at his own needy behavior.

If Trey liked the first more, he didn't linger on it. He reached for Cassidy's hand and dragged him to the door. Once inside, the noise of the band assaulted them, along with the scent of liquor. Yet Cassidy's sweet fragrance was there, teasing Trey's sensitive nose and keeping his wolf on edge.

His wolf whined at the delay as Trey glanced up and down the passageway checking it was empty before hauling Cassidy toward the restrooms. He breathed a little easier at finding the accessible restroom empty. It had more space, and when he locked them in, he spun Cassidy around, pressing his chest to the door. Without preamble, he yanked down Cassidy's sweats and groaned at the sight of his bubble butt atop slim hips and lean legs. Slick glistened in the overhead light as it slid from between the tight buttocks.

"Fuck, look at you," Trey groaned, having to take a firm grip on his cock to get himself under control. Confined in his jeans, it throbbed painfully against the fabric.

Cassidy folded his arms in front of his face, glanced back, eyes so bold. The blue so dark they added to the allure when it came with the knowledge Trey had caused the desire in their depths. When he tilted his ass at Trey in invitation, then smirked right before he braced his head against his arms, Trey struggled not to go into a rut.

Holy fuck!

The howling of his wolf matched the long drawn out growl and he ripped at his fly and dragged his jeans and boxer briefs down enough to get his cock free. He shuffled forward and pressed his chest against Cassidy's back, feeling him shudder, his ass lifting higher.

Bending at the knee, Trey's lips touched Cassidy's ear. "Hold the fuck on." It was all the warning he gave as he took hold of the notches above Cassidy's hips and angled him just right. In a practiced move, he thrust deep.

"Yes," Cassidy cried out in a strangled moan, surely letting all the other shifters in the bar with good hearing know what they were doing.

The ease at which he sank in gave Trey a moment to wonder who had fucked Cassidy to make him so loose. He slid in like a knife cutting through butter. He hated the thought of someone touching Cassidy, as did his wolf, who snapped, his teeth descending.

No.

Yes.

I will stop right now! He would, despite what it cost him. The ache in his jaw receded at how serious he was. Claiming a mate in such a way? No, Trey would never allow that. He exhaled and then inhaled through gritted teeth. It didn't help when all he could scent was Cassidy's sweetness, his slick, driving him to fuck. To knot the little omega.

Cassidy drove back and bucked forward, fucking himself on Trey's cock. For a second, Trey didn't move, uncertain how to react to this different side of Cassidy. He usually let Trey lead and would passively take what he offered.

"So needy," he murmured, rotating his hips in a slow move, keeping his cock deep. "This what you want?"

His lips remained next to Cassidy's ear, his hot breath blowing on the flushed skin. Cassidy twisted sideways to look at Trey.

"More. Fuck me," he begged. "Don't tease me. I need to feel you."

The depth of meaning behind the fire burning in his gaze made all the air in the room disappear. It was too much and not enough all at once, and Trey lost it.

He pounded into Cassidy, listening to the sounds that poured from his mouth as he begged for more despite the sweat slicking their clothes to their bodies. Dark patches appeared on Cassidy's sweater as he undulated and writhed against the door. His hands remained away from his cock, just how Trey preferred. He could make Cassidy come with a hard fucking, but usually what drove him wild was Trey's knot swelling in his ass.

His body was ablaze with the need to come. To pump his seed deep in Cassidy. He reached around and took hold of Cassidy's hard length, feeling the hot, silky shaft pulse against his palm. He held it loosely as he thrust deep enough that his knot pushed past the rim of muscle guarding Cassidy's ass, stretching it.

The mewling came as Trey went still, his cock spurting deep as his knot grew, expanding until he fully knotted Cassidy. He was now Trey's captive, pinned to him, making him Trey's in the most elemental way. Everything about it filled Trey with a possessive desire, one he could normally contain. Except in this moment, when Cassidy's head landed on his damp shoulder, and Cassidy buried his face into Trey's neck, he could only go along for the ride as a passive observer.

Emotions, the kind he knew would fuck him up, came in heady waves as cum spurted over Trey's fist and Cassidy mouthed at his neck, his body rippling in the throes of his passion, crying out his name. "Treyyyy!"

Hearing the way Cassidy called his name like this, like he was a god, never grew old and his body accepted what he denied his heart.

"We need you, boss," Kendrick called through the door while hammering on it. "So hurry the fuck up."

The interruption cut through the euphoria like someone had thrown icy water onto a fire to quell the blaze. Trey cursed internally when he felt Cassidy stiffen against him, his heaving chest slowing as he continued to hide his face in Trey's throat.

He heard Kendrick stomp off. Not that they were going anywhere just yet. His body would decide that. They would remain knotted together for some time, and it was why he avoided doing it—when he could. The intimacy of it left him weak.

He kissed the side of Cassidy's head. "Ignore him."

His words never got rid of all the tension, Cassidy was far too easy to read.

"Look at me," he murmured softly. It took a moment and there, in Cassidy's gaze, was the vulnerability that made this about more than sex. As they were, Trey gave in and kissed him, not the frantic kiss they'd shared when Cassidy had shown up. This was slow and measured. He sipped at

Cassidy's sweetness, lingering over each kiss. He wasn't sure how long they kissed like that, but Trey was unnerved to notice his knot had deflated and he had wrapped himself around Cassidy—cuddling him close.

Shit. What the fuck am I doing?

This was so not part of their agreement. He couldn't gauge what Cassidy's reaction was to his behavior because he was doing his level best not to look at him.

"Fuck, boss, we got an issue out here!" Kendrick shouted, sounding pissed and giving Trey the perfect excuse to leave.

"I gotta go," he muttered, still not looking Cassidy in the eye as he straightened up his clothes. Their scent and the state of him were a dead giveaway, but all Trey could do was sigh and tuck his sticky cock away. After a quick wash of his hands, he swung around at the sound of the lock and door opening. Cassidy waved a hand in the air, then disappeared.

Trey's eyes slammed shut, and he groaned aloud. What the fuck had made him give in and cuddle Cassidy? He'd clearly made the wrong move, because Cassidy was never the first to leave. Trey usually left first. It was self-preservation.

"Cranny is losing his shit out here... holy fuck boss, it smells like an omega brothel in here." Kendrick glanced down the passageway and back to Trey, frowning. "Somethin' ain't right with this picture!"

"Button it," Trey snapped, not in the mood to go a round with Kendrick right then.

Kendrick shrugged massive shoulders, the light of interest not waning. "Whatever. But now you got your head out of your pants, I need you to have a fucking word with Cranny." Kendrick, a huge bear shifter who had worked for Trey since he had opened the bar twenty years ago, was the only one who got away with speaking to Trey this way.

They'd been friends for too long to do bullshit.

"What's he losing his shit about now?" The lion shifter who worked at Darling Ranch, the biggest one in these parts, could be tricky to reason with when he'd had too much liquor. "Is Ethan in?" Ethan managed the ranch and was very capable of dealing with his ranch hands.

"Nope, he left earlier." Kendrick ran a hand through his gray, cropped hair, a sign of his frustration, which made Trey feel bad for leaving him to deal with shit he shouldn't have to. "Zippy said some shit about lions being lazy and—"

"And because Zippy is all about getting a rise from Cranny, they decided they'd do it in my bar like fucking usual." Trey, too impatient to use the hand drier, shook them, then wiped the residual wetness off down his jeaned thighs, ignoring how sweaty he was and that there were cum stains on the back of the door. He would deal with it later, because Kendrick was right, it did smell like a brothel in there now.

He locked it from the outside so no one could go in, then his mind switched to Cranny, who occasionally broke more than a few chairs when he was pissed. With the band in tonight, Cranny would have no issue tossing folks out of their seats.

"You should just bar the pair of them," Kendrick pointed out, following close behind Trey.

He glanced back and rolled his eyes. "I tried that, remember? Then Cranny gives you that whole fucking 'I'll change my tune', only for Zippy to get in a snit over some shit and take it out on Cranny. Why they don't just fuck each other and be done with it, I don't fucking know."

Kendrick coughed to disguise his laughter.

"Fuck you."

"You're just a big softie, admit it." The bear's grin was all fucking teeth.

He pointed at him. "You're fired."

"I heard that a thousand times before. Who else would put up with your shit?" There was a big enough pause for Trey to know what was coming. "Oh yeah, that would be Cass."

Trey never replied, and he stomped into the busy bar, pushing up his sleeves, ready to use Cranny as an excuse to burn off the anger directed at himself for giving in to his needs. He'd deal with the 'Cassidy issue' later, when his mind wasn't so full of how it had felt to hold the chick or *how right it was.*

Chapter Three

Cassidy

Being inside his cabin gave Cassidy too much time to think about the night before, when he could smell Trey in his space. All because of the clothes he had tucked under his pillow—gross—because he couldn't make himself launder them, along with everything else, that morning. He was an adult; he did not need to explain his behavior or justify it to anyone but himself.

But you are.

I'm an adult, he pointed out to his animal side, because it was all Cassidy had right then.

Then act like it and go tell the hunky wolf what we want.

No.

Everything got mixed up and he suspected it was because of his heat.

It isn't.

Shut up.

He should have waited for today to visit Trey, then he wouldn't be feeling like this.

Unnerved?

Was that the best way to describe it? It was as if he was waiting for the other cowboy boot to drop. Never a good thing, in Cassidy's opinion. He wanted to believe he had pushed Trey to act differently because of his heat—or the lingering effects—which could more than account for the intimate touching and kissing. Yes, Trey touched him intimately and kissed him, but not like he'd done last night.

Was that the residual heat effect on Trey?

Really, this is pointless. Go ask him.

Honestly, why don't you cluck off!

Fine, I will, but I will not be there when you need to offload.

Blessed silence followed, and Cassidy got left with his own thoughts once again.

Trey had fucked him hard, just like he had demanded. As usual, there was dirty talk. The stuff that gave Cassidy material to get off on between trips to the bar. With how addictive Trey was, he limited himself with how often he could visit.

Trey had an apartment above the bar. Had Cassidy seen inside it? Nope. Not once had they gotten beyond the restroom in the bar. Cassidy wondered if the reason why was how needy he got.

Although he wasn't the only one. Trey could be as bad as Cassidy, and he didn't have heats. And as much as Trey talked about letting others watch them—wolves, he had heard, had no inhibitions when it came to sex or sex in public—he always made sure they weren't visible when they fucked.

Last night, with how Cassidy was, he would have let Trey fuck him over the hood of his truck. And Cassidy wasn't sure how he felt about that in the cold light of day, now his hormones were better under control.

The knotting... although Trey did like to knot with him, it wasn't a frequent thing. When they had done it before, Trey had *never* kissed him softly. Had *never* wrapped his arms around him and held Cassidy like he was precious. Wasn't that more than causal fucking? This question was fucking with his head.

If it was just sex, then what was different about last night? Was it his hormones? Or something else? The unanswered questions roaming around Cassidy's mind were why he had been up early, using the time to finish knitting Lynda's jumper.

He blew out a shuddery breath and stomped out of his cabin, clutching what he'd made, needing a distraction and knowing exactly where to get it. His girls. He knew the other ranch hands laughed at him because they didn't hide their amusement. They thought he was a little bizarre with how he treated his chicks.

Did he care?

Heck no.

He bred chickens; he was a rare breed himself, not that he could shift, but he didn't care—mostly. The breed of his family was Plymouth Rocks, and they could lay pink and purple eggs. Cassidy had long since resigned himself to how his family viewed his lack of ability to change, so he had substituted them for a family that was much more appreciative of him.

He tipped his cowboy hat as he walked across the back paddock when he noted Ethan astride a stallion. Cassidy had half convinced himself to be in love with Ethan when he first arrived on the ranch, through a program that the owner had started for youths in foster care.

Ethan, tall, dark and athletic from working with the horses, was a sight that could stop any hot-blooded person in their tracks, especially when he was astride a horse. He was a specimen of pure hotness. Mostly, he was shirtless when working with the horses, which was nearly all the time. The man was a horse whisperer. They'd had many troubled horses come to the ranch, and Ethan—to Cassidy's knowledge—had never failed to help a single one.

Bare chested and sweaty with hay stuck to him, Ethan rode to the edge of the paddock, stopping a distance from Cassidy, who held up his hand for the horse to smell him. Horses were sensitive creatures. "Mornin'."

Ethan tipped back his hat as he examined Cassidy with a serious look. "Mornin' Cass." His nose wrinkled, then smoothed out, and a smile appeared. "You're over your heat."

Not so much a question, more an observation, but Cassidy nodded. "Yep, I'm just off to see how Sunny is getting on with my girls."

Ethan's laughter rumbled out, startling a bird resting on a tree branch. It squawked its displeasure and flew off into the cloudless sky. At this time of day, it wasn't too hot to make it unbearable, so it was pleasant to stand and chew the fat.

"You and your chicks." Ethan eyed what was in Cassidy's hand. "That another knitted thing for one of them?" His voice held a wealth of humor that also made his dark brown eyes glow in his deeply tanned face.

Giving a shrug, Cassidy matched Ethan's grin. He never took offense because he loved his ladies. "They're my girls, what can I say?" Cassidy held up the purple knitted garment. "Lynda will look great wearing it with her little tutu of feathers."

This time Ethan rocked on the bare back of the horse, his laughter making the horse take some side steps. "You'd brighten the darkest day, Cass." He wiped at his eyes as he continued. "It'll be interesting to see what our new guests will make of your chicks."

"New guests?" Cassidy couldn't recall any mention of their being guests coming. They offered different ranch experiences for the city folks. It was usually too hot at this time of year for anyone to want to come and learn about being a ranch hand.

"Silas, his brothers, and their assistants are coming for a week, maybe less. They haven't quite decided yet, from what Silas mentioned when we spoke."

"They are?" Cassidy asked, wide eyed. As far as he knew, none of the owner, Silas Starling's brothers, had been to the ranch, except for Booker. There were eight of them, and Silas's parents, Lane and Derick, had adopted five of them, if the gossip on the ranch was to be believed.

Silas, who Cassidy knew loved working on the ranch despite working for Starling Enterprises, one of the largest fashion businesses out there, of late had all but disappeared.

"When was this organized?"

"A few days ago. They arrive Monday." The stallion whinnied and flicked its head. Ethan stroked over the mane, "It's alright boy," he murmured softly, and the horse settled.

"I'll leave you to it. If you need me to do anything extra, just shout."

At the nod, Ethan tipped his hat back into place and, holding the horse's mane, squeezed his thighs and they took off. Horse and man as one, fluid and stunning to watch as they moved in unison. Cassidy had never ridden bareback, but Ethan seemed to prefer it.

The squawking coming from the direction of the hen-houses brought Cassidy's attention to where he'd been heading before he'd stopped. His grin spread at the welcoming committee of Lila, Lisbeth, Luna, Lottie and Lana.

"They's my girls," Cassidy crooned as he walked to the large enclosure where the chickens roamed free. Their henhouses were tucked back close to a large barn, so even when the weather turned, the inside remained mostly dry.

Sunny appeared from inside the barn carrying a large pail full of eggs as Cassidy's little chicks made a beeline for him, squawking and chirping in delight.

"Cass, I thought you had the day off today?" Sunny said, projecting his voice to be heard over the welcome the girls were giving Cassidy, his gaze on where he walked so as not to tread on any of the Seramas chicks.

They had several breeds, and the Seramas' were the smallest. The teacup puppies of the chicken world. Sweet and lovable with curly feathers, they were smaller than a coke can and came in a wild assortment of colors, feather patterns, and feather types. They also made great pets because of their loveable nature. Some of his girls often spent the night in his cabin when he was feeling the need for company.

"I am, but I was awake, and I've done all my chores." Cassidy held up the knitted purple top he'd made for Lynda. "And as I finished this, I thought I'd come and see if it fits."

Sunny stifled a giggle. "You know, you're probably the only dude on the planet who would knit clothes for his chickens."

With a small shoulder shrug, Cassidy sat down on the dirt and grinned when the chicks immediately climbed on to him. "If you love someone, you gotta treat them right," he murmured, stroking carefully at their feathers. "Isn't that so, girls?"

The clucking started in earnest, and Sunny's giggles got drowned out.

Cassidy spotted Lynda coming out of the barn, and she held all his attention as she stalked majestically towards him. The La Fleche breed unfortunately made Lynda and her sisters a bit satanic-looking. With jet-black feathers and fleshy little devil horns, they stood out in the crowd. This breed of birds was more aloof around people, and, unlike the others, they didn't follow their owner around. Lynda knew who the boss was, and it wasn't Cassidy.

She tolerated him and his crazy notion to make her look less satanic and more pretty. "Look what I got for you, Lynda."

She pecked at the purple wool several times and then lowered her head in approval. "I knew you'd love it," he crooned.

"You know it won't make her look—"

Cassidy shook his head, not shifting his gaze from Lynda.

"Don't be mean," he said softly to Sunny, and to Lynda, "to my special lady. She has feelings too." He carefully pulled the knitted top into place, pleased with how it fit.

"Perfect."

Sunny sauntered off, mumbling under his breath, loud enough for Cassidy to hear, "Sometimes, I worry for you."

He lifted Lynda up to look her in the eye. "There's nothing to worry about, is there?"

Cassidy was sure he could see amusement in her eyes as she squawked, then flapped her wings to show it was time to let go if he didn't want to be pecked in the eye. When she sauntered off, proudly displaying her knitted top, Cassidy beamed with satisfaction, his mind focusing on what color to make Letta's sweater.

Chapter Four

Cassidy

The arrival of the newcomers the day before had brought much excitement to the ranch and not all because Silas was there for the first time in months. A couple of months ago, his parents chose to retire, rather suddenly, or so it seemed. Silas hadn't even mentioned anything to Ethan, who got the same shock as everyone else at the announcement.

It was that Silas had come with all his brothers. There'd been a lot of speculation as to why they would all come on a team building retreat to the ranch when they were now all in charge and working together at Starling Enterprises.

Cassidy, unlike the other guys who worked on the ranch, had paid little mind to the new arrivals. He wasn't interested in them other than being polite and friendly. Some of the single ranch hands took an interest in any new arrival, in case they'd be up for a bit of fun. The only one Cassidy wanted to catch the eye of and have fun with was Trey.

You already caught his eye.

Thanks for reminding me.

You're welcome.

"Bubba, come on darlin', you gotta wiggle that cute backside outta there. You're makin' me late, and Ethan will have my hide, never mind yours. I have a group to work with today," he coaxed.

The loud squeaking noises that followed, along with some grunts, did not sound amused.

Bubba, a Kunekune pig, was tiny *and* a Houdini. Highly intelligent, he had figured out how to escape the pig pen to come up and visit Cassidy. He didn't come every day, but because he was so small and couldn't climb the steps to the porch, he would go under and squeak and grunt loudly to get Cassidy's attention. The problem was, he was tiny, but his belly wasn't, so he'd get stuck under the porch. Like he was now. Cassidy was too big to go under and get him, so he had to talk Bubba out of the tight squeeze.

"Excuse me. Erm, can you tell us where we can find Cassidy?"

In a fluid move, Cassidy rose from where he was crouched, looking at the group of men all dressed in jeans and plaid shirts that didn't make them look any more like a cowboy than if they'd worn a sign saying it.

He tipped his cowboy hat. "I'm Cassidy. They call me Cass around these parts."

"I'm Hollis," said the man in front of the group. He pointed to the other men one by one, "Bowie, Wilder, Monty, Frey, Isley, Lennon and that's Ziggy." They all raised a hand and offered him a smile, some more nervous than others.

"Nice to meetcha. I'm sorry, I'm runnin' a little behind as Bubba is stuck. I've been tryin' to coax him out from under the porch steps."

"Bubba?" Frey asked, coming closer and crouching down to peer under the steps.

"A Kunekune pig I hand reared. He's real clever, just not when it comes to judgin' gaps, which gets him wedged under my cabin, more often than not." Cassidy released a heartfelt sigh.

"I could shift and go help him, if he wouldn't freak at my fox."

"Why, that's mighty kind of you. Bubba's not frightened of other animals." Cassidy lowered his voice. "He got little pig syndrome."

Bowie came forward, looking intrigued. "What's that?"

"Why, he believes he's bigger than all the other animals."

"Is that bad?" Bowie sounded worried.

"Nope, he's a small pig with a big attitude. The other animals don't hold it against him 'cause he don't mean no harm."

While he was talking, Frey stripped off his shirt and Cassidy noticed the mating mark before Frey shifted. He peered up out of his jeans as he wiggled to climb out. A moment later he sniffed under the porch, then he made a small vocal noise that was cute as the fox himself before he crawled under.

There was some grunting and more squealing, then Bubba darted out between Cassidy's legs, his little black body wiggling with excitement. Cassity laughed, scooping Bubba up to kiss the dirty snout. "How many times I gotta say, don't go under the porch?"

The hairy snout rubbed Cassidy's cheek as Bubba recounted just how happy he was to see Cassidy. Then he noticed the crowd of men, and he grunt-snorted a greeting at them, causing them to giggle.

"He's cute," Bowie murmured. "Do you think he'd mind if I stroked him?"

"He's not a horse," Wilder pointed out.

"He likes bein' petted." Cassidy strolled closer to Bowie. "Hold out your arms." When he did, Cassidy laid Bubba in the crook of Bowie's arm, getting a shy smile in response. "See? He'll stay in the crook of your arm all day if you let him."

Cassidy chuckled as Bubba rested his hairy chin on Bowie's forearm and closed his eyes, making a snorting noise that was all pleasure when Bowie stroked a gentle finger down his back.

"Frey, do you need a place to shift and dress in private?" Hollis looked about as Frey sat next to his clothes, a few cobwebs stuck to his brush.

"He can use my cabin, if that suits?"

Frey walked up the steps and waited at the door. Cassidy got beaten to collecting Frey's clothes by Ziggy.

"Door's open, we'll wait here for you. Then I can take you up to the henhouse to meet my girls."

"Your girls?" Lennon asked, blushing as Cassidy gave him a wide smile.

"Yep, my chicks."

Wilder went to Bowie and gave Bubba a scritch behind his ears. "I like this when folks do it to my raccoon."

"Don't I know it," Bowie moaned. "The last time you wouldn't let me stop for over an hour. My arm felt like it didn't belong to me."

Cassidy listened to them chatting, seeing easily they were more than folks who worked together. They were friends. Some were quieter than others, except they always included everyone when they were talking. A family. That's what they were.

Frey came out of his cabin, his hair a little messier than it had been. "I never thought my first job was gonna be helping a stuck pig." He grinned cheekily as he came down the steps. "Wait till I tell Emmy I got to recuse a pig."

"Emmy?" Cassidy assumed Frey must be talking about his mate.

"My daughter. She's at home with Derick and Lane." His smile dipped a little before it brightened. "They're having a blast with her from the number of pictures I'm getting. Do you wanna see?"

"Say no." Wilder gripped Cassidy's arm. "Don't let him drag you into that trap of cuteness. It'll make your whole day disappear."

"As Ethan would have my hide for that, what say we get started and then you can show me when we take a break?"

"Wise move," Hollis muttered, giving Frey a look that suggested he behave, which totally by-passed the dude when he pulled out his phone and flashed a picture of a cute baby at him.

"She's a cutie for sure,"—he started walking—"and will be a real heartbreaker when she gets bigger."

Frey showed him several more pictures, getting groans from the others, though they all wore the same sappy grin as Frey when he flashed the phone at them, before they had put Bubba back in the pigpen and got greeted by the girls.

"Has that chicken got a tutu on?" Isley peered over the fence, his eyes so wide Cassidy struggled to keep from laughing at the obvious shock. He went to open the gate, and the chickens rushed towards him.

"That one's got a sweater on," Lennon whispered. "Oh, and that one."

"Where would you buy something like that?" Bowie questioned, leaning over the fence to get a closer look.

Cassidy grinned, used to the questions, though these were politer than some. "I knit the sweaters for them and make the tutu's. My girls like to look pretty." He shrugged causally, heading through the gate.

The noise they made as they gathered around him, like a pack of wild hens, halted those following him. "Now come on girls, you know that ain't how we greet visitors."

The squawking and wing flapping came down a notch.

Lulu made a beeline for Bowie, who hovered in the gateway. Cassidy didn't get to say a word as Bowie got down on his knees and offered her his finger. "She's so tiny."

"She's a Seramas frizzle. Frizzle means she got all those pretty wild colored curly feathers."

Lulu pecked and fluffed out her feathers because she knew Cassidy was talking about her. "I breed various kinds. There's a market for chicken feathers."

When Cassidy first started working on the ranch, there weren't many chickens, and they'd roamed free. As his animal side was a chicken, and he had an affinity for them, he had seen an opportunity to start a breeding program of different breeds that were popular for eggs, feathers, and meat.

"Feathers?" Bowie asked, as three more of the ladies went over to show interest in him.

"Feathers. They have a lot of keratin, a protein which, when harvested from the feathers, can help balance plastic structures and make the plastic stronger. It's big business, if only on a small scale for Darling Ranch." He gave a sheepish smile. "I really just love having lots of little chicks of my own."

"What type is the one in purple?" Frey asked, finally braving stepping through the gate, side stepping Bowie and the chicks.

Cassidy didn't need to look because only one of his girls wore purple. "Lynda is a La Fleche."

"She looks... interesting," Wilder muttered, lifting his feet, watching the chicks as they darted around him.

"Ya mean the satanic-looking feather display?" Cassidy whispered. "It's why she prefers to wear her sweaters."

Lennon muffled a giggle behind his hand. Cassidy got it, she was a wild-looking chick.

Cassidy continued to talk about his girls, grabbing pails and handing them out. "We need to collect eggs first, then clean out the henhouses before feeding."

He glanced at the group, seeing enthusiastic smiles. He was sure that would change when they got to the chicken poop, but it was a good start because no one had run off like the chap from the month before. The guy from New York had made rude comments about his girls, then called Cassidy crazy. His chicks had gotten affronted and sent him packing in a barrage of peeking and wing flapping. "That okay?"

"We are in your hands," Hollis answered, apparently for everyone.

"Great, then let's get crackin'."

Chapter Five

Trey

"What's with you?" Kendrick wiped at the bar counter, his gaze on Trey as he turned to the cash register. "You look like you swallowed a hornet, and it's stuck in your throat. It don't have anything to do with a certain someone who is getting lots of attention, does it?"

"I don't know what you're talkin' 'bout," Trey muttered, keeping his eyes from tracking Cassidy, who had arrived half-an-hour earlier with a group of men that Trey had never seen before. The bunch were mighty friendly with how they were touching Cassidy.

The small blond was the worst culprit.

"Liar," Kendrick fired back. "That color green ain't never suited you."

Trey nodded to where Cassidy stood at the side of the dance floor, too annoyed to stop himself from asking, "Who are they?"

"How would I know?" Kendrick's powerful shoulders shrugged while he moved down the bar to serve a guy who signaled him.

By the glint he'd caught in Kendrick's gaze, Trey figured he was purposefully trying to piss him off. He knew that, with how busy the bar was, he should just let it be.

"You're the gossip," he countered, loud enough to be heard over the music, too wound up to let common sense rule.

"Might be so,"—Kendrick grabbed a bottle of the fancy IPA and opened it—"but where would be the fun in telling you when I can watch you sweat over Cassidy?"

The dude Kendrick was serving was also unfamiliar, and from the smile Kendrick gave the guy, he was interested in more than serving him a drink.

Although their town had a couple of bars, Trey had worked hard to make Ranch-Down popular with all age groups, even making it family friendly on certain days. That meant that he knew a lot of folks and having so many unknown faces in the bar at once was pretty uncommon.

Trey lifted his middle finger when Kendrick took the cash off the guy, giving him a flirty wink, and went to the cash register. "After Friday, isn't it time you fucking admit there's something real goin' on between you two?"

Kendrick said it loud enough to draw the attention of numerous regulars, so Trey resisted getting into it in front of an audience. There was no band tonight, just the jukebox next to the dance floor, which was at the back of the bar, near the small stage Trey had added several years back to cater to the younger crowd. The young folks got to dance, but everyone else could still carry a conversation over the music. Despite Bayfield having a pretty decently sized population, it was still possible to start a rumor at night fall and have it spread to damn near everyone by morning.

It didn't matter anyway because he already knew Kendrick's thoughts about the situation. After Trey had dealt with Cranny on Friday night, he went back to the restroom to clean up their mess. It hadn't taken a genius to work out that the cum stains on the floor could only have come from Cassidy's ass. That alone was a huge dose of reality about how carried away he'd gotten. Only once before had they gone bare and that had been after a particular night where Trey had spent hours watching Cassidy dance. He had been so worked up, much like Friday, and forgotten himself. He'd sworn it would never happen again. In a moment of weakness and self-doubt, he'd gone back out to the bar and told Kendrick everything.

There was so much information about matings between divergents and shifters that Trey wanted to be careful, for Cassidy's sake. It wasn't that he was averse to having pups, he just felt it should be a joint decision, not something done in the heat of the moment. He shook off his lack of regret he felt or how desperate his wolf was to get close enough to

Cassidy to scent him. To see if their chick was indeed pregnant. Because something else had struck Trey too, after he'd stripped that night; Cassidy's scent. It was sweeter, more tantalizing. There was only one thing that could alter a scent and that was a heat. Had Cassidy been going into his heat?

Recalling how he'd felt when he had fucked Cassidy, his teeth ground together at the idea he might have been Cassidy's second call of the night, if indeed he was coming into a heat. There were places where omegas could go to find alphas if they needed one. Is that what Cassidy had done? Cassidy didn't seem to be fucking anyone else from the ranch or in town that Trey could tell. Not that he watched Cassidy all that much.

Liar.

A bill got waved in Trey's face and he blinked the stunningly attractive man into focus, blushing at being caught unawares, looking into space—at Cassidy. He met a green-eyed gaze that held a touch of wildness. For a brief moment, Trey got the odd feeling he was staring at a wounded animal.

He shook off the feeling when the guy smiled at him, adding to how beautiful he was. The man was insanely attractive. Trey acknowledged it, but the guy held no appeal for him, though he could admire the lean, lanky frame wrapped in denim and plaid. A cowboy hat covered his hair, but sat in such a way Trey could tell he wasn't a genuine cowboy.

"Do you have a decent bottle of red wine?" The voice wasn't cultured, but it had a quality that suggested some time in a private establishment where folks talked proper.

Trey nodded, leaning on the bar, fascinated for reasons he couldn't say. "Got a decent Barolo, but it'll cost more than that twenty you're flashing at me."

The man's laughter was rich and smooth. It matched the sexy grin that spread over—Trey decided—a far too attractive face. "If I was flashing at you, it most definitely would be worth more than a twenty." The smirk was full of confidence. "And finally, something decent about this hell hole. I'll have a bottle, please. And if you like, you can join me?"

Unsure about the decent comment, it took a second to register the offer. Before Trey could decline politely, Cassidy was there, giving the guy a look he couldn't translate.

"Jupiter, I see you've introduced yourself to Trey."

Once again, Trey struggled to gauge what was going on with Cassidy from the way he smiled at Jupiter.

"No introductions as yet, but the night is young."

There was no way to miss the sexual overture in Jupiter's voice, but Trey couldn't tell if Jupiter aimed at him or Cassidy.

Jupiter held out his hand. "Jupiter Starling."

"Jup, there you are! Why the hell didn't you wait for me?" asked the stranger that Kendrick had winked at a moment ago.

Jupiter ignored him, and Trey took the hand, surprised at feeling work roughened skin against his.

When Jupiter finally answered, lingering over the handshake, he didn't look at the other guy. "Because, Rue, you were fussing about having a cold shower and I was in need of a *stiff* drink!" He stared at Cassidy when he emphasized the 'stiff'.

Trey would have wondered how Rue had arrived before Jupiter if his wolf wasn't snipping and getting worked up at Jupiter eye fucking Cassidy.

Cassidy made a noise in the back of his throat. "If you can let go for a moment," he snapped, his aquamarine eyes swirling with an unusual temper, "I'll have a glass of water. I'm parched."

Jupiter chuckled and dropped Trey's hand, his gaze shifting between them. "It seems you are. Care to join me for a glass of wine?"

Trey swallowed the 'fuck no' that wanted to come out of his mouth, seeing Kendrick eyeing them all with amusement. These were Silas Starling's brothers and Silas contributed a lot to the town and Trey liked the man. So he kept the scowl off his face and went to get the water and the wine, believing the evening, which had taken a wrong turn when Cassidy showed up with a group of over friendly men, was now somehow worse. There was a deep ravine up ahead and he couldn't see it. Despite that, he continued to head in its direction!

Chapter Six

Cassidy

Shocked by his own sudden burst of temper, Cassidy eyed Jupiter like one would a rattlesnake. With caution.

"You got the hots for Trey." The way Jupiter said it didn't come out as a question, more an observation.

Cassidy watched Trey's back as he walked to the wine cooler, unsure if he should respond. "We fuck, that's all."

It was crude, but Cassidy felt out of sorts and was thrown off by his urge to warn Jupiter off. The Starling brother's PAs had plenty to say about Jupiter and his sexual exploits. The man had a reputation and a smile the devil himself would want.

"Is that so?" Jupiter sounded intrigued and there was a glint in his eyes as he stared at Cassidy. "Want to put that theory to the test?"

"What do you mean?" Cassidy asked, interested despite himself, when Jupiter gave him a kind of knowing smile that made no sense.

He didn't answer immediately as Trey returned with a glass of water and an open bottle of red wine. "Want me to leave the bottle here?" Trey asked, placing Cassidy's glass in front of him.

"Perfect, and I'll have two glasses, or will that be three? The offer still stands if you care to join us?"

The smile he gave Trey set Cassidy's teeth on edge. He wasn't the jealous type. He knew he wasn't bad looking, that in the right light he could look pretty good, but Jupiter was on a whole other level.

Had the man set his sights on Trey?

The PAs spoke about Jupiter being dominant, so he couldn't see how Trey would interest Jupiter, but maybe a trip...

"No! Sorry, we're busy, but enjoy it."

How Trey sounded brought Cassidy from his thoughts and he stared at Trey in shock, working on figuring out why he would be rude to Jupiter. It just wasn't in Trey's nature, even when pissed he was always polite.

Jupiter offered over a fifty-dollar bill and Trey snatched it and walked off, casting a look at Cassidy that came over as worry. But why, Cassidy had no clue, or none that made any sense.

After Trey returned with Jupiter's change and left to serve the next customer, Jupiter poured himself a glass of wine from the open bottle. He took a sip, and a groan of appreciation followed. "Would you like a glass? It's good."

Cassidy didn't drink, he came to Trey's bar for two things, Trey and dancing. "Nah, but thanks."

Jupiter took another sip and looked to savor it. "Your loss."

"'Bout what you were sayin' earlier. What were you gettin' at?" Although Jupiter appeared a bit of a jerk, Cassidy had good instincts and so did his chicks. When Jupiter had wandered around the ranch and found Cassidy working, Jupiter had come in and gotten a true introduction to Darling Ranch from Cassidy's girls. They had loved on him, even Lynda hadn't been averse to getting acquainted.

After another sip, Jupiter eyed Cassidy with a serious look. "I like you—"

Cassidy held up his hand. "Sorry, I'm not interested."

Jupiter chuckled, not looking in the least bit put out at how blunt Cassidy was. "Not in that way. But Trey does."

Fascinated despite himself, Cassidy came closer, keeping his voice down. "How do you know that? Like I said, we've been fuckin' for two years, and he's given me no sign it's more than just sex."

Until the last time.

Did that count?

Jupiter raised one plucked brow. "None? I doubt that very much. The man can't take his eyes off you. And if he continues to look at me the way he is, I'm sure I'll end up in a smoldering pile of ash."

Cassidy's heart bounced in his ribcage while he tried to resist the urge to turn and see what Jupiter was getting at. Only his piqued interest got the better of him, and he looked out the corner of his eye to see what—if anything—Jupiter was getting at.

Possessive?

Was that what he could see? A look Cassidy had seen in the bathroom mirror when Trey fucked him against the wash-basin.

Was Jupiter right? Did Trey have feelings for him beyond the sexual chemistry they shared? His breath caught in his chest at the hope that came before he could squash it back into the place he kept it hidden.

He shook his head. "I think you got it wrong."

"Shall we see?"

"How do you think you're gonna do that? 'Cause you ain't touchin' me, just to be clear."

Jupiter placed his glass down next to Cassidy's untouched water as Kesha's song, *Take It Off*, played on the jukebox. He slid off his stool and offered his hand. "Wanna dance, cowboy?"

The dance floor quickly filled with cowboys, the song a popular one to dance to and entice someone to take off their shirt in time to the lyrics. Which could be fun.

Although he loved to dance, he'd avoided this particular song because the only person he wanted looking at him shirtless was on the other side of the bar.

Pulse hammering in his ears, Cassidy took Jupiter's hand, feeling more than a little out of his depth, and threaded through the crowd, feeling the weight of Trey's gaze on him. It didn't help with the nerves in the pit of his belly when he danced to the beat of the music.

His shoulders moving, he let go of Jupiter's hand and started following the steps of the guys lined up on the floor, moving in time.

A fluid dancer, Cassidy lost himself in the music, singing along. *"There's a place I know if you're lookin' for a show, where they go hardcore and there's glitter on the floor."* When Cassidy looked through the crowd and snagged Trey's gaze, he sang to him, *"and they turn me on when they take it off. When they take it off, everybody take it off."*

He reached for the hem of his T-shirt and ripped it off over his head to the chorus of *right now (take it off), right now (take it off), right now (take it off), oh-oh-ooh-oh.*

Jupiter was there dancing with Wilder and Ziggy, two of the PAs, but his shirt remained in place whereas Wilder was topless, and Ziggy's shirt was open and flapping about his tattooed body as he danced and spun in time to the music.

Cassidy grinned, enticed, when Jupiter spun around him, blocking his view. Jupiter gave him a broad wink and then moved behind him, hands taking hold of his hips and, though they weren't ass to groin, anyone looking from the front would think they were.

He didn't have a chance to protest when Trey vaulted the bar into the crowd in a move that left Cassidy dry mouthed and unbelievably turned on. His brain playing catch up, Cassidy found himself marched through the crowd, off the dance floor, out of the bar and up the stairs leading to Trey's apartment.

If he wasn't so shocked, he would have done a damn happy dance at Jupiter's intuitive instincts.

"W-what... what's wrong?" he finally managed to eek out past his growing excitement and arousal.

Trey spun around, kicked the door shut and then spun back, his eyes flashing danger in a way that made Cassidy take a step back, wanting to test the wolf.

Trey's steady fingers went to the buttons of his shirt and undid them as he stepped closer to Cassidy.

"What's wrong?" Trey rasped in a gravelly voice, his head tilting to the side a fraction, his eyes narrowed on Cassidy, making him swallow hard. "No one gets to touch you but me."

From the way Trey said it in that possessive tone, Cassidy was ready to bust a nut, and Trey hadn't even touched him yet.

The atmosphere in the apartment buzzed with sexual tension and, though they had great chemistry together, it had never felt like this.

"Who do you belong to?"

Cassidy eyed Trey and did something that went against his very nature. He lied. "No one."

Emerald eyes glittered as they narrowed further. "Is that so?" Cassidy shivered at the dark intensity, his cock painfully hard. "Then why is your slick dripping out of your ass, begging for me to fuck you?"

The shirt landed on the floor and Trey toed off his cowboy boots, not taking his gaze off Cassidy as his hands went to his belt buckle. Leather slapped against leather as he whipped it out and flung it to the floor. "Come here."

"No." Cassidy baited the wolf, riding the wave of euphoria and power that came from the knowledge that Trey was acting like this because of *him*.

Before he could register what Trey would do next, Cassidy found himself pinned to a wall, arms restrained above his head, Trey's mouth on his, devouring him.

Wet, hot and all tongue and teeth, Trey ate him like a starving wolf. Cassidy groaned in delight at the feeling of power growing with each greedy kiss exchanged. He had no recollection of how they ended up naked or with him pinned to the wall on Trey's cock, his legs wrapped around his slim hips, ankles hooked. Facing him was a novelty and Cassidy reveled in the feeling. Arms free, he cupped Trey's bristly cheeks and held him to kiss him with all the feelings that were swamping him. When Trey's knot started to stretch him, Cassidy whimpered and mewled into Trey's mouth as he came in furious bursts over the wolf's stomach.

"That's it, mark me as yours," Trey demanded, wrenching his mouth free, gusty breaths hitting Cassidy's face.

Their gazes locked and Cassidy's teeth ached at the demand. He came forward, tilting Trey's head back, and struck his jugular in the throes of his release. Blood filled his mouth, and he swallowed hungrily, his world narrowing to just one thing: his wolf.

Heat filled his ass as Trey came in great shudders, the knot expanded fully, forcing yet more cum out of Cassidy's aching balls. "Mine," he rasped when he released Trey, swiping blood from his lips.

The wolf's eyes were there, looking at him, when fangs appeared. Cassidy's heart hammered as he lifted his head back to expose his throat in submission. "Bite me," he commanded throatily.

"Are you sure?"

Cassidy cupped the back of Trey's head and dragged him closer, understanding once more that he held the power. "Yes. I was sure the day I agreed to let you take my virginity and nothing has changed," he confessed, watching Trey's shock turn to hot, potent possessiveness.

"I was your first?"

"You are my only," Cassidy whispered shyly.

"Oh, fuck!"

Teeth struck his throat and Cassidy groaned in rapture, his vision flicking in and out before everything snapped into a new clarity. A clarity that Trey was his, and nothing could change that.

A sob rose, then another. Overcome with emotions, Cassidy clung to his mate, feeling his tongue lick over his claim bite. "Mine," he sobbed, "you're mine."

Joined as they were, they weren't moving, but Trey cuddled him close and kissed his tear-stained cheeks. "We are, my little chick." He rested his forehead against Cassidy's sweaty one. "We are—eternal.

Chapter Seven

Trey

Trey rolled over the bed and buried his head into a pillow, blocking out the sounds of someone pounding on his front door. Didn't they know they were playing Russian roulette, waking him before he was ready to get up?

Taking a deep inhale, his head popped up, and his blurry eyes opened at the aromatic scent of Cassidy. The night before flooded his mind with such clarity, a heat of arousal flowed through him. He mated Cassidy.

We did.

I don't need a fucking reminder.

He didn't, because the second Cassidy had confessed to them being the only one to touch him, nothing on this planet could have stopped him from claiming his little chick.

More banging came, which he ignored as he rolled to sit up and flick on the lamp beside the bed so he could get a better look at the messy—empty—bed. Where was Cassidy? The blackout curtains didn't give Trey any clue to the time of day, but if someone was hammering on his door—and unless they wanted to die—it had to mean it was after eleven.

"Get your ugly ass out of bed," Kendrick called from outside.

"Fuck off," he shouted back, his hand going to the tingling skin at his throat while his wolf pranced about his mind giddily, ready to give chase after Cassidy.

What's with you?

Didn't you scent him?

What?

The sound of the door rattling and Kendrick using his key got Trey to roll, naked and pissed, off the bed. He quickly looked for something to cover up his neck, not ready to have this conversation until he spoke to Cassidy. What was important right then was getting rid of his friend, who was now in his space, moving around in his kitchen.

"What part of fuck off don't you get?" he called out, rummaging through the pile of clothes on a seat.

He sniffed at a sweater and threw it on before finding a pair of sweats to slip on. Barefoot and grumpy, as Cassidy had left without a word while he was sleeping and didn't seem to have left a note, he stomped to where Kendrick was filling his coffee machine.

"You better have brought breakfast." He glanced out the window behind Kendrick, trying to figure out the time of day.

"It's nearly lunchtime, you ass." Kendrick measured out coffee beans while Trey went to the cupboard where he kept his cereal. He dragged out the box and grabbed a bowl, milk and a spoon.

Bowl filled, he leaned against the counter and ate to keep himself occupied, watching Kendrick.

"You're pissed," he observed.

Kendrick didn't even bother to glance in his direction. "I shut the bar down last night when you did a disappearing act. I was hoping to get a fucking lie in only Des rang me 'cause you hadn't shown up to set up for opening."

Chewing on the cereal that was supposed to be cinnamon but tasted more like vanilla, assessing the situation and his friend's mood, Trey eyed Kendrick with interest. "You had company."

"I did, and thanks to your lazy ass, I had to leave when things were just getting interesting." What he meant by that, Trey didn't want to think about. Kendrick preferred more than one man in his bed at a time and liked to direct them so he could watch before he got involved.

"Sorry."

Kendrick pointed a stirrer at him, looking at him for the first time. His lips parted in what Trey suspected was going to be another tirade, only his eyes dropped to the collar of his sweater. He could hear the wind whistling through

Kendrick's blown mind. Trey didn't need to be top of the class to know that Kendrick had noticed his claiming bite.

When, seconds later, he took a step towards him, his lips remained parted. Eyes stretching wide, he let out a strangled noise. Trey had to resist tugging the sweater higher to cover himself.

Don't you dare cover it.

"What the ever loving fuck! Did hell freeze over? Did fancy pants at the bar last night steal your fucking sanity?" Kendrick rasped, sounding winded as he continued to stare, making Trey battle the urge to squirm.

"Just stop—"

"Stop what? You let Cassidy claim you!"

Trey was sure that every person within a one-mile radius heard Kendrick as he shouted at him.

"That's none of your business," he snapped, but Kendrick had already walked off in the direction of Trey's bedroom to glance inside.

"Where is he?" He looked back at Trey, his nose wrinkling, possibly from the heavy scent of sex, looking more than a little worried. "Tell me it was consensual?"

"How fucking long have you known me?" Trey fired back angrily, his throat clogging at his friend thinking he'd mate with someone without consent. "He fucking bit me first!"

And okay, he'd kind of asked for it—sort of. Not that he wanted to change a thing, because once he and his wolf had decided they wanted Cassidy, it was a done deal. In the cold light of day, maybe he should have talked about it and not done it in the heat of passion. Especially with how riled Trey was at Jupiter touching Cassidy. How sexy Cassidy looked dancing on the floor, shirtless, his chest glistening under the lights.

If Trey thought hard, he could still feel the lingering rage at seeing the other man's hands on what was his. It was an asshole thing to think. To believe. But fuck, if it wasn't the truth. Cassidy was his, just as much as he belonged to Cassidy.

"He did?" Kendrick questioned, coming back to the counter, not sounding in the least convinced.

"Yes, he did." Trey plonked his spoon into his half full bowl of cereal, having lost his appetite, and placed it on the counter. All he could think about was going to find Cassidy so they could talk, and ask why he left without so much as a 'goodbye'. "Now, if you've finished havin' a go, you can leave."

The coffee machine started to spit and bubble as the scent filled the kitchen. Kendrick went back to the pot, shaking his head. "Nope, I'm not going anywhere until you explain how you went from never wanting a mate—only last week—to being mated."

Trey groaned and took the doctored coffee Kendrick offered him. Seeing his friend's concern was the only thing stopping him from throwing him out. "What's to say? You know I was interested in Cassidy—"

"Fucking is what you kept saying you were doin'."

He ground his teeth together. "That might be so. But I ain't fucked anyone else in more than a year." Or two. Trey had tried to fuck a dude that hit on him after the first time he'd touched Cassidy, only he couldn't get hard. His wolf did not like the guy's scent at all. He should have known then the writing was on the wall.

You did, you're just real good at pretending is all.

Thanks for the update.

You're welcome.

Asshole.

Sometimes, his wolf was a real asshat!

He had told no one, not even Kendrick, about what was going on, despite the conversation they'd had after the lack of a condom. Instead, he had led Kendrick to believe that he was still hooking up with other guys, so he got why his friend was acting this way—kind of.

Kendrick sipped the dark brew and eyed Trey. "You ain't had sex with anyone since Cassidy"—his eyes narrowed over the mug—"have you?"

He sagged against the counter, seeing it was pointless to pretend when Kendrick knew him better than anyone. "No, I tried once, and I just couldn't…"

"Get it up," Kendrick finished, smirking.

Trey gave him the finger. "Smug asshole."

"Always. So what you gonna do now?"

"What do you mean?" Trey asked, unsure what Kendrick was getting at.

Kendrick sighed and rolled his eyes at him over his coffee mug. "The mating bit is easy. But Cassidy lives up at the ranch. You live in town above the bar. He works at the ranch. Early mornings mostly, from what I see. You work here, late nights typically. So how is all that gonna work?"

Kendrick laid out all the things that said life was about to get real tricky and raised the concerns about why Trey had stayed with hook-ups for so long. "We'll figure it out."

They would... *wouldn't they*?

Chapter Eight

Cassidy

"Lynda, stop pecking at Lila, you know she don't like it," Cassidy gently reprimanded while continuing through the large barn, collecting eggs and listening to his ladies' chatter and squawk at him.

He understood that they'd be a little unnerved by his scent. Could anyone wash off a mating scent?

Stop being silly. Our mate's scent, his blood, is part of us now.

Yes, but does it mean I'll smell like him all the time? I haven't had a chance to shower because you wanted five more minutes to cuddle with Trey before we had to leave.

You wanted to make up for the cuddles we've missed, so stop making out it's just me.

Cassidy chuckled at being called out. Yes, he had wanted to linger. Was it wrong? It was so new, but as dawn broke, he had reluctantly slipped out of Trey's bed, his mind circling around how it was going to work. To Cassidy's way of thinking, things had started out great.

His mate, it turned out, was a big cuddler. Although was it cuddling when he starfished the bed and therefore lay sprawled over Cassidy at the same time? He didn't care, because waking that way was something he hoped to get used to.

That would require you to actually hang around to speak to our mate.

I have to work.

They had this argument all the way to the ranch and, it seemed, through all his morning chores. Pail in hand, he bent to run his hand down Luna's feathers when she pecked at his leg, looking for a little attention.

Then the squawking started in earnest as she rubbed her beak up and under his jeans to his ankle. "What's this all 'bout, my sweet girl?"

He placed the pail down and scooped her up in his palm, bringing her up to his face. Her speckled feathers fluffed, and he grinned at the pretty show she was putting on for him.

Luna was a sweet girl who liked lots of attention. He had hand reared her after finding her struggling to get out of her shell. Smaller than the other chicks, she'd failed to thrive alone. Cassidy didn't like to intervene with nature, but would never neglect a chick who needed a little help-ing hand.

"Can you scent my mate?" he murmured as he met her gaze. The noises she was making got louder.

Many thought chicks didn't have a great sense of smell, but they'd be wrong. "It's alright, you're still gonna be my favorite girl."

That seemed to calm Luna, who rested her beak on top of his thumb, giving him what he'd describe as a flirty look. No one would convince him otherwise. He knew his chicks; they were all flirts, in the worst way.

He kissed her beak, giving her what she wanted.

"Do they like that?" asked a quiet voice from his right.

He glanced over at the man watching him. For such a big man, the guy sure was able to move around unnoticed.

Cassidy recalled Bowie had chosen not to come to Ranch-Down the night before when most everyone else had. The team building retreat was most definitely divid-ed into two camps. Those loving it and those who hated ranch life. Bowie appeared to be in the first camp.

"Mornin' Bowie. My girls love the attention," he glanced down at the chick, who was quietly watching the exchange. "Don't you, sweetheart?"

She puffed out her feathers and Bowie giggled, step-ping closer, being careful not to trample on any of the other girls running around at their feet. Cassidy liked the guy for that. Some weren't as careful with their booted feet in the large barn.

"She's real pretty." Bowie lifted a finger and gently put it in front of Luna's beak, then grinned at Cassidy when she nipped at it.

"What are you doing hiding out here?"

Both Cassidy and Bowie looked at the man standing by the doorway. Tall and blond, the guy looked a little out of place in the messy barn in his crisp shirt and pressed jeans. The cowboy hat did little to suggest Kari fitted in on the ranch, unlike Silas.

Last night, Cassidy had gotten to socialize with almost all the visitors. Kari certainly was the calmer of the twins. His brother Kodi had a more volatile nature. Cassidy wasn't one to judge others, but he had noticed how Kari used his influence to help defuse his twin's short fuse. The rest of the brothers, Booker, Rue, Laken, and Taylin, had attempted to get the most out of the experience. Jupiter would never be a rancher, that was for sure, despite his affinity with the animals.

Booker and Taylin were the two who appeared to enjoy what the ranch had to offer the most, along with their mates. Frey was Booker's mate and Cassidy found he really liked the cheeky fox. Taylin was mated with Hollis, who was a little more buttoned up than Cassidy was used to. The guy wore a serious expression most of the time. He had hoped to get to know Hollis a little better the previous evening, then Jupiter...

Gave Trey a little incentive.

Is that what happened?

He worked to shut down his train of thought and answered for Bowie, when he didn't appear to know how to reply. "My harem were just sayin' 'hi' to Bowie."

Deep laughter got the chicks scattering and Bowie blushing. Luna didn't so much as move a feather, her contentment clear.

"Is that so?" A playful smile appeared as Kari threaded his way towards them, also being careful.

"Do you need a hand in here? I'm sure Bowie and I could be helpful. The others are heading out for a ride."

Something passed between the two men, and Cassidy felt a little like an intruder. "Don't you wanna go? I'm fine here."

"No, Bowie isn't keen on riding a horse."

Cassidy nodded at Bowie, giving him a reassuring smile. "Being on a horse can be a little scary. The ground can seem a way aways from you, for sure."

He placed Luna down and petted her before nudging her towards the tray of feed he had put out when he'd first arrived.

"I'm happy to stay here and help," Bowie murmured, not looking at either Cassidy or Kari, his cheeks a bright pink. "Do I get to help put their cute little outfits on?"

"If ya wanna," Cassidy said with a wink. "My girls do love to look pretty for visitors. But first we gotta finish collecting eggs, then muck out."

Cassidy enjoyed his morning with Bowie and Kari. Once Bowie got over his initial shyness, he was an enthusiastic helper. It had been fun watching him dress the girls in their sweaters to go outside. Kari had helped, but mainly he'd watched Bowie, which was cute.

Although Cassidy's morning was busy and he'd missed grabbing something mid-morning to eat, he felt satisfied he had explained the workings of the ranch to Bowie. It turned out the guy had endless questions when the other PAs weren't there to vie for attention. By the time he left with Kari to go get lunch, Cassidy's girls had trailed after Bowie, much as they did to him.

Sweaty and more than a little grimy after mucking out the stables, hunger drove Cassidy up to the main bunkhouse despite it being long past lunchtime. Here, the workers could find hot food at any time of the day and, if they wanted, company. Too occupied with how his stomach clenched with the need for food to consider going back to his cabin, Cassidy had one boot inside the bunkhouse when he realized that he should have given his situation—that he hadn't showered after leaving Trey's and his newly mated smell—some thought.

Inside the overly warm, busy bunkhouse, it was too late to leave as his nose wrinkled while he sniffed, trying to scent himself. Was it just him that could smell Trey on him?

"Holy cowboys, what is that smell?" Ande, a horse shifter farrier, called out with a laugh.

"Cassidy," replied Brook, who was sitting closest to the door. Suddenly, those who'd been busy eating and minding their own business seemed a lot more interested.

Cassidy had long since given up thinking about what folks thought about him, he just didn't want them gossiping about his Trey situation.

Mates, not a situation. He's our mate. We are mated. Mated to Trey.

How many ways do you have to say it?

As many as it takes for you to go strut your stuff and show off in front of this lot.

Cassidy's amusement grew as he shook his head and strode up to the array of heavenly smelling dishes laid out on the counter that separated the room from the kitchen where Petey and Orion spent their day. The two men were mates and loved to wind up the ranch hands for fun. Cassidy could see the second Petey's gaze found its mark—him.

"Well I never, Cass done gone and got himself a mate," Petey announced the second he got a good whiff of him, his gaze on Cassidy's throat.

I've got a mate. Trey is mine. Guess what, I'm mated to a hottie.

All of it fit the occasion, yet none of that fit how monumental it felt to Cassidy. He had secretly yearned for this. Now he just didn't know how to share the same way he had with his chicks. They didn't judge. The men in the bunkhouse would.

At his lack of response, the noise in the bunkhouse grew with shouts and laughter.

"One of your gal's got your tongue?" Stark, an enormous bear of a man who loved to tease and always wore a mischievous grin, asked when he came and stood way too close to Cassidy and sniffed. Cassidy felt his hot breath on his skin, and immediately went to draw away, only to freeze when he inhaled a very familiar scent...

"Get the fuck away from my mate." A threatening snarl made the hairs on Cassidy's arms rise.

The situation in Cassidy's jeans was wholly different. They became way too snug for comfort as he spun around and met Trey's hungry stare.

Oh my.

Chapter Nine

Trey

It hadn't taken Trey much persuading to get Kendrick to step in and work the bar for him today so he could go find Cassidy and set him straight on a few things.

Like leaving without so much as a word.

Showered and dressed, Trey headed out of his apartment with one goal; hunt up Cassidy and find out why he'd not bothered to wake him or leave a damn note before he left. Wasn't that the polite thing to do? The more time he'd thought on it—dwelled—the need to find Cassidy had grown like an itch he couldn't quite reach to scratch.

Mates.

They were mates.

Trey, who never had expectations before, had them now. It was lowering that he was more needy than his omega mate. He would never have believed it of himself. Except, here he was, ruminating over the fact Cassidy left without so much as a kiss goodbye. *That just wasn't on.*

He cringed at his own stupid self, and how he could not persuade himself differently on the drive up to the ranch.

It was new, this mating thing, but he was dang sure that sneaking out of bed and leaving a mate was not the done thing.

Yep, he was like a damn broken record. Problem was, he couldn't find the needle to pick it up and stop it playing. So he had driven at breakneck speed to the ranch to have a discussion with his mate about expectations.

There, finding Cassidy had proven harder than he'd expected. First, Trey had never set foot on the ranch. He'd had no need until now. Second, the place was fucking huge, and it had taken several wrong directions to get him to the bunkhouse. He'd also received several amused looks when he had questioned the ranch hands about Cassidy's whereabouts.

Even scenting Cassidy hadn't worked initially with how many other smells there were to distract his wolf. So when he finally found Cassidy, he had a wealth of pissedoffness going. Then, seeing Stark getting cozy with his mate was the last straw. His wolf was all for tearing the big fucker's nose off his face for getting it too close to Cassidy's neck.

"What did I say?" he growled around his fangs, scenting his mate's arousal, pushing back his cowboy hat to get a better look at Stark. "Get the fuck away from my mate." His own body reacting to Cassidy's scent, further pushing Trey to act and show his dominance.

Cassidy was the first to move in the way too quiet, tension filled room. "He didn't mean no nothin' by it."

"Is that so? Then what the fuck was he doing with his nose in your neck? Didn't look like nothin' to me." His wolf flashed in his eyes, issuing a threat to all in the room.

"Trey, we don't want no trouble here." This came from Orion, who came around the counter, nudging Stark away from Cassidy and keeping his distance, too.

Orion was the biggest shifter in the room and, though Trey had no quarrel with him, his need to get everyone away from Cassidy would not abate. There, under everything else he could smell, was something that amped up his protectiveness to a level it had never reached before. Not known to turn away from a fight, and neither was his wolf, Trey eyed everyone as a potential threat to his mate. He had busted more than one head from Darling Ranch when they had gotten too rowdy at the bar. This situation was different, and Trey had no control over what was going on inside him.

"Neither did I until Stark started sniffin' my mate."

Stark finally found his tongue. "I was messin' around, Trey. Windin' Cass up, just friendly like. Nothin' more." He held up his big, meaty hands in defense. "I ain't interested in your mate, I swear."

To Trey's mind, Cassidy was the only man in the room worth looking at, so it stood to reason the others would be interested. Naturally, that meant Stark was lying to him. He stepped deeper into the room, his boots thudding ominously on the wood.

Those who sat at tables watched with avid interest. Trey would be the talk of the town, and he didn't give two fucks as long as everyone got Cassidy was his.

"I think it's time we left." Cassidy came forward, his pheromones doing a number on Trey, who found himself propelled out of the bunkhouse and marched towards a row of cabins, sitting back in the distance.

"We can talk about this in my cabin," Cassidy finished, not stopping as he steered Trey away from the men.

That was fine with Trey. He wanted to have this conversation about expectations in private. He'd speak to the ranch hands when they visited the bar just to make sure they got what was happening here. Cassidy was his.

In silence, they reached a set of steps up to a porch that had a small porch swing gently swaying in the breeze. Once inside the cabin, Trey turned to face Cassidy, his thoughts lining up to be explained.

Cassidy was on him the second the door clicked shut. Heat poured from Cassidy's body. He smelled of the ranch, and all the smells that entailed, but none of it mattered when his mouth crushed Trey's. The shock of this dominant side was like a flash fire to Trey's need. It poured gasoline over it, making it blaze. This might not be exactly what he had wanted this morning, but it was so much fucking better.

He groaned and grappled with Cassidy's clothes, needing to get to his skin. His hat tumbled to the floor along with Cassidy's torn T-shirt and his belt. The buckle hit something on the way down, causing a clatter. Trey noticed none of it. His entire world was the man in his arms and the clawing need to prove to himself Cassidy was his.

They wrestled each other out of their clothes and collapsed against the first flat surface they arrived at, which turned out to be a wall. Cassidy wrapped his legs around Trey's waist, plastering himself against Trey. Nothing mattered except touching, claiming his mate. The second Cassidy's mouth moved down his throat, Trey lost it.

"Bite me," he urged, his desire for the connection wouldn't let go, fueled by how Cassidy was behaving.

"Fuck, yes," Cassidy groaned. His sharp teeth sank deep into Trey's flesh and sent shudders of lust through him, like a river breaching a dam. He adjusted his stance to get his cock under Cassidy's balls. The slick from Cassidy's ass allowed him to thrust and sink balls deep in one swift move.

Trey pinned Cassidy to the wall, driven on by the sounds Cassidy was making, and grunted at the sudden force of his release when Cassidy bit harder, clinging to him in desperation. When Trey's knot expanded, cum spurted between them. He growled his pleasure, sinking deep into it, letting go of all reality except for Cassidy.

A hot, sweaty and sticky mess, Trey chugged in air, his nose buried deep in the crease of Cassidy's throat and shoulder, feeling his pulse beat. Feeling the connection between them thrum under his skin as Cassidy's body continued to quake, despite Trey's knot reducing and allowing cum to seep out.

Cassidy ran the tips of his work-roughened fingers up Trey's sweaty back. "Wanna tell me what brought that on? Not that I'm complain'."

Trey swallowed a sigh and gave himself a couple more seconds where he was, inhaling deeply, loving how Cassidy melted against him when he brushed a soft kiss against his rapid pulse.

"You left without sayin' a word," he murmured eventually, knowing nothing but the truth between them would do. Still, he couldn't quite meet Cassidy's gaze. "Or givin' me a kiss."

He expected laughter. Amusement.

What he got was a sound that made him look Cassidy directly in the eye to figure out what he was hearing. The sound came with a sense of warmth from Cassidy. "You wanted me to kiss you goodbye?"

Hadn't he just said that?

He prayed that Cassidy thought the heat in his cheeks was to do with what they'd just done and not that he was—most definitely not seven shades of—embarrassed. "Yep."

"I... oh..." Cassidy scratched at his eyebrow, the one that was quirking up, adding to the adorable lopsided smile that appeared. "You did?"

He came in and cupped Cassidy's cheeks, holding his stare. "I did. Pissed me right off when Kendrick woke me and you hadn't even left me a note or nothin'." The hurt came out with his confession.

Cassidy was sensitive, and his smile disappeared. "I hurt you. Shit, I never meant to, I swear. Just I hadn't been expectin'... you know what, then my alarm woke me, and I didn't wanna wake you... in case..."

Trey kissed him when his lips trembled and his eyes became dewy, buckling Trey's knees and upsetting his wolf, who stomped about like a toddler having a fit.

Fix it.

"I know," he whispered against Cassidy's mouth, sneaking another kiss. "I suppose we should have talked about expectations and shit before the other stuff."

Cassidy snuggled closer, seeming not to care about the cum that was drying on them. "I suppose." He peeked up at him from under long eyelashes, worry evident in his gaze. "You don't regret it, do you?"

"Fuck no," Trey exclaimed quickly, bringing Cassidy back in for another kiss. Now he had the taste of him, he found it hard to stop kissing him. "You are the best thing to ever happen to me."

Cassidy sighed against Trey's mouth. "Same goes." The kiss was a gentle coaxing of lips against each other. The dreamy quality of it left Trey's heart aching and his body responding once more. Cassidy chuckled and his ass clenched around the hardening shaft. "It looks like we have a growin' problem you could use some help with."

"Seems we do." He rolled his hips. "Know anyone that could help a cowboy out?"

The gleam in Cassidy's eyes set Trey's heart rate to kick up its heels and head for higher ground. He nuzzled his way up to Trey's ear. "I believe I do."

Cassidy's ass squeezed as he adjusted his legs, hooking his ankles over Trey's ass to keep them around his hips, making it hard to contain the low moan of approval. Trey slid his hands under Cassidy's plump ass, bringing him closer, keeping his attention on the flushed man, who looked sexy as fuck. This side of Cassidy was most definitely worth exploring. "And who would that be?"

Cassidy gave him a fucking irresistible, playful look. "Your mate," he whispered, right as he claimed Trey's mouth.

What more could he say, when actions were so much more fitting?

Chapter Ten

Cassidy

Talking was mostly a lost cause because every time Trey got within three feet of Cassidy, there was no way to keep his hands off and his clothes on. The day before, Trey had stayed up on the ranch in Cassidy's cabin. Cassidy had cooked them a meal after the three hot sweaty bouts of mind blowing sex. He could almost believe he was coming into his heat with how he was behaving.

When he'd cooked, had they talked then? Absolutely impossible when Trey had his hands wrapped around Cassidy's dick the whole time, encouraging him to work faster. Had they talked when they were eating? Another nonstarter when they had eaten in bed, and mostly off each other's bodies.

Cassidy's ass was aching, and he worried that there might be something wrong with him. When he'd woken Trey to kiss him before heading out this morning—after shower-ing—to get on with his daily routine, he had none of his usual enthusiasm for his work.

Could a mating change a personality?

"What's with the long face?" Ethan leaned against the fence around the paddock Cassidy was working in, resting his forearms on the top, looking at him.

A black jacket hung open over a gray T-shirt, and Ethan's Stetson was the same color as his jacket. It shielded his eyes, but Cassidy picked up his unease all the same.

"Do you think mating changes who you are?" he asked, voicing what was on his mind, knowing Ethan wouldn't take offense that he hadn't answered his question. They had worked together for seven years, and Ethan was someone the ranch hands could talk to, regardless of him being the boss.

Dark brows arched as Ethan pushed back his Stetson to scratch at the side of his head. "I heard there was a ruckus in the bunkhouse yesterday. So it's true then, you an' Trey are mates?" There was nothing about his stance that suggested it could be a problem.

Yet...

Cassidy dusted off his hands and grabbed a rag from his back pocket to rub the sweat off his face. Today he wore a backward baseball cap to hold back his bangs. Tucking the rag back into his pocket, he grabbed his water canteen to take a drink, thinking about what Ethan could have heard. "Sorry 'bout that."

"Nothin' happened, did it?"

Cassidy shook his head. "Nah, not the way you mean."

A palomino stallion on the other side of the paddock took notice of them. Anywhere Ethan was, if there were horses nearby they would trot over.

"What way is that?" Ethan asked, digging a hand into the bag Cassidy had on the fence holding apples and carrots. He held up a carrot, his gaze remaining on Cassidy.

"Trey was upset with me." Even as he said it, Cassidy remained disconcerted at how he had hurt Trey's feelings. It was not in his nature to be careless like that.

A loud whinny was accompanied by the thump of hooves as Hero came to a stop and nipped the carrot out of Ethan's hand more delicately than one would expect. "There's my boy."

Ethan's voice held all the affection he had for the animal when he reached up and stroked the shining mane. The horse's head flicked towards the hand nibbling him.

"What did you do?"

Ethan's question made Cassidy refocus. "I left without kissin' him or leavin' a note."

A deep bassy laugh got Hero's head bobbing and his tail flicking. Ethan divided his attention between the horse and Cassidy. "I never had Trey down as... the clingy kind."

Cassidy's brow furrowed, not liking how Ethan said the word 'clingy'. "He's my mate."

"I get that." His eyes gleamed with amusement. "Is this why you're thinkin' a matin' changes ya?"

"Not really, I was meanin' me."

"So Trey's always clingy when you fuck in the bar's restroom?"

Blushing hard enough to make sweat gather on his top lip, Cassidy found it hard to hold Ethan's gaze. "That ain't none of your business."

"Then maybe you should have fucked some place no one could hear you," Ethan said matter-of-factly. "I ain't mated, so it's hard to say what changes and what doesn't. Though to my thinkin', everything changes 'cause you got someone else to consider, whether you like it or not."

Cassidy frowned once again at how Ethan made mating sound like an inconvenience. It most definitely wasn't that.

"It ain't like that," he muttered in frustration. "And I'm not bein' clear."

"Then explain yourself."

"I'm not sure I know how to," he confessed, when none of his thoughts made sense.

"Is this where you're hiding?" Jupiter's smooth, sexy voice interrupted them.

Ethan groaned, just loud enough for Cassidy to hear it, despite the smile he offered Jupiter as he wandered from the direction of the big house. Those who stayed on the ranch for the team building experience usually bunked in the cabins. Cassidy had heard that Jupiter had moved up to the big house.

"I ain't hidin', just runnin' a ranch is all," Ethan offered affably. Cassidy didn't miss the tightness of his jaw or the slight narrowing of his eyes.

"Seems like hiding to me," Jupiter replied, striding closer, his hand lifting for Hero to sniff. "Cassidy, looks like the experiment worked for you."

"Experiment?" Ethan asked, his eyes narrowing further as they moved from Cassidy back to Jupiter. "What're you talkin' about?"

Hero nudged at Jupiter's shoulder, nuzzling at his immaculate button-down. Jupiter's head tilted and rested against Hero's in a relaxed move.

Cassidy glanced at Ethan, who wore the same expression of surprise as Cassidy did. Horses were sensitive creatures, very empathic and able to pick up things that other animals couldn't sense. Jupiter had an affinity with most of the animals on the ranch, which Cassidy had witnessed firsthand, despite how much he had complained while doing the team-building activities.

Hero was Ethan's horse, and he rarely paid attention to any of the visitors to the ranch. Ethan couldn't miss the special attention Jupiter was receiving.

"Cassidy believed that Trey and he were just fuck buddies, but it was easy to see that was not the case." The devilishly handsome smile Jupiter aimed at Ethan brought with it a rosy glow to his cheeks. "It only took me placing my hands on Cassidy's..." he paused long enough to gain a frown from Ethan, "hips to get Trey to vault the bar." He winked at Cassidy. "A hot move I'm sure he followed through on."

"Am I interrupting somethin'?" Trey drawled.

Cassidy glanced to the side and tried to work out what he was picking up from Trey. He looked a bit rumpled in the clothes he'd arrived in the night before, which had spent the night lying on the floor in a heap. His damp hair curled around his hat, with the brim sat low enough to shield his expression. "No."

Trey came to the fence, grabbed the post and in a move Cassidy would absolutely never tire of seeing, vaulted it to stand next to him. Trey's freshly showered scent didn't disguise Trey's arousal, which automatically triggered Cassidy's. Not that it took much these days.

Hero glanced at Trey and whinnied in disapproval.

Jupiter chuckled and scratched Hero's neck. "I think that's my cue to leave." He tipped his hat at them and strolled off.

"Trey... we don't want no trouble, ya hear me?" Ethan's stance changed as he stood to his full height, giving Trey a warning look.

"I'm not looking for trouble as long as folks understand who Cassidy belongs to," he asserted in a low growl.

Cassidy didn't feel conflicted. Maybe he should, given how Trey was behaving, but that would be a double standard because Cassidy felt the same. When he looked at Trey, he wanted others to know that the wolf was his. He'd pined for this and now he had it, he would not be shy about it. Though that didn't mean there wasn't a conversation that still needed to be had.

"That good for you, Cass?" This was what made Ethan a good boss.

"It is," he asserted, turning his attention to Trey. "'Cause same goes."

The smile that slowly spread as Trey stepped to Cassidy meant that was all he could focus on. Heat warmed his body and his heart beat harder.

"You finished?" Trey asked.

"Shouldn't you be askin' me that?" Ethan muttered through his sniggers.

Trey continued to hold Cassidy's gaze. "Is he?"

Hero trotted off, head flicking, when Ethan laughed. "It seems so."

"Let's go."

Guided out of the paddock, Cassidy shut out Ethan's continued laughter, glancing sideways at Trey. His brain became scrambled, much like the eggs he ate for breakfast, by the sexy smell coming from Trey.

Once more in his cabin, the door shut, Cassidy eyed Trey, whose fingers went to the buttons on the rumpled shirt. Only then did he notice a couple were missing.

"Is mating all about sex? Not that I'm complainin'." He wasn't, but at some point they needed to talk... *didn't they*?

Chapter Eleven

Trey

Despite the arousal coming from Cassidy, Trey was anxious as hell, which was why his hands dropped to his sides. Narrowing his eyes, he searched Cassidy's expression. He really did want to talk, but every time he was within touching distance of Cassidy, the need for him left little room for anything else. Trey did something that was way more difficult than it had ever been before and took several steps back. When that didn't seem to help, he reached to open the door and inhaled.

"You okay?" Cassidy asked, coming towards him, his brows drawn together. Trey stepped outside onto the porch.

He offered a tight smile. "I'm all good, if you keep your distance."

Cassidy's crestfallen expression set off Trey's wolf, who growled at him. "I didn't mean it like that." He rubbed at his bristly jaw in frustration. "The need to touch you makes me crazy. It always did, but now I can't seem to talk sense to myself and keep my hands at bay."

A familiar lopsided smile appeared, and it struck Trey that he was never gonna be able to resist Cassidy. Two years of pretending things were causal between them because they only had sex meant fuck all to how much he'd always wanted this man. His claim on him happened long before he sank his teeth into his flesh. It was galling to realize he had wasted so much time when he could have spent it with Cassidy figuring this out.

"I'm not sure I'm seein' a problem." Cassidy's aquamarine eyes glittered with confidence and grabbed Trey right by his balls.

"Cass, you're killin' me. If we're gonna talk, then I can't get too close to ya." He held up his hands, taking a step back. The porch creaked under his boots when Cassidy moved towards him.

The sexy motherfucker grinned and tucked his hands into the front pockets of his jeans, eye fucking him. "I'm listenin'."

Trey had to move, or he was going to have Cassidy inside his cabin and never let him back out. He eyed the porch swing and sat on it. The other cabins didn't seem to be occupied as Trey listened out, searching for anyone close by that might overhear them.

When satisfied they were alone, he returned his attention to Cassidy. He had kept a little bit of distance between them and was leaning against the porch rail, watching him. "How do you see this workin'?"

Cassidy's brows tugged together as he held his gaze. "We're mates."

Trey shook his head. "It ain't that simple, is it?" He pointed out at the land stretched out before him. "You live here on the ranch, work here. I live in town and own a bar that requires a lot of my time. How do we merge those things to make this work?" He asked all the valid questions Kendrick had asked him, to which he still had no answers.

The frown lines grew deeper, and Trey got an unsettled feeling in his gut as Cassidy lost his confident pose. "What are you sayin'? That we won't be able to make it work?"

Trey got up and went to Cassidy, wanting to remove the uncertainty he could see in his expression, and took hold of his shaking hands. "No, that's not what I'm sayin'. But it's gonna take some workin' out. If I'm honest, Cass, I don't like the idea that I'm gonna have to leave soon and go to work. That I might not get to have you close by when I finish work."

Cassidy eased his hands from Trey's and came close to slide his arms loosely around his middle, meeting his worried stare. "I can come to town tonight."

"What 'bout tomorrow and the day after that? This thing we did..."

Trey felt Cassidy's body tense. "What?"

"It might not have been planned, but I want to make plans so that we're together in the same place, not miles apart."

His cheeks darkened, as did his eyes, and Cassidy tightened his hold, laying his head on Trey's shoulder. He rubbed his nose up the side of Trey's neck in a move that made Trey feel all kinds of things. "I want that, too."

The whispered response eased some of Trey's tension. "Okay... okay. How's 'bout you pack some clothes to leave at my place and come to town with me, we can get somethin' to eat, then you can eye fuck me while I work. How's that, for starters?" They had to start some place.

The kiss Cassidy placed against Trey's bouncing pulse gave him a fluttering feeling in the pit of his stomach. "I could do that. I'll have to leave early in the mornin'. Is that gonna be alright for you?"

Apprehension was there, but with it was hope. "As long as you don't go forgettin' my kiss before you leave, we'll be fine."

Cassidy chuckled and lifted his head. "I'm sure I can manage that."

Trey had a week of shifting his schedule around, with Cassidy doing the same, and as much as they'd been able to see each other every day, the nights had become an issue. Trey's wolf was pretty sure Cassidy was pregnant. The nights sitting at the bar, waiting for Trey, weren't good for their little chick, especially when he had to get up at dawn for work.

Cassidy didn't say a word about the pregnancy, so Trey held back the need to go into protective mode. That was something he was dealing with, though maybe not totally when Kendrick was ragging on his ass about his mood swings. He kept hold of those in front of Cassidy when he didn't want his mate feeling he was to blame.

He had gotten Cassidy to agree and go back to his cabin to sleep, so he got rest. Trey fucking hated waking alone and being sensible. He wanted to head to the ranch every night and wake Cassidy up to...

"If you keep wipin' at that like it's pissed ya off, the thing is gonna need replacin'."

Kendrick's voice broke through Trey's brooding, and he eyed his friend, thinking he'd be a better target to take out his frustration on. The beer taps were so shiny, Trey could see his grumpy expression on them.

"Whatever ya got goin' on in that head of yours, forget it. I ain't in the mood for a boxin' match when we gotta open up in half-an-hour," said Kendrick.

"You sure? I ain't the only one in a fuckin' mood." He wasn't. Kendrick had been off for the last few days, which wasn't like him. "Your new fuck buddy leave town?" Trey hazarded a guess.

"What you know 'bout that?" Kendrick snapped back, now wearing a similar expression to the one Trey wore.

"I ain't heard anythin'. Just putting the numbers together, is all."

Kendrick eyed him for several seconds before he cursed. "That guy Rue, him and one of the others in the group he came with. We got a thing goin'. It was... interestin'."

Trey arched his brow, taking the distraction. "Interestin' how? And I didn't notice anyone hangin' with the rhino shifter."

"Did you notice anything other than Cass sitting at the bar eye fuckin' ya?"

Trey grinned, his good mood returning despite knowing Cassidy wasn't coming in later. "Why would I want to notice anythin' else?"

"Fuck you!"

"Only person doin' that with me is Cass," Trey pointed out because he could, and it made him feel like a damn pack leader. "So Rue, he gone back to Hazardville with Silas and his brothers?"

Kendrick gave a disheartened sigh, and Trey narrowed his gaze on his friend. "You're interested in more than fuckin'," he exclaimed, not giving Kendrick a chance to answer.

"It seems this"—he lifted his hands, air quoting—"wantin' more, seems to be catchin'."

Trey slapped at the bar. "Holy fuck, man, I never thought I'd see the day—"

"Don't go fuckin' gloatin'. You were the one pissed off 'bout Cass not comin' in tonight."

There was no arguing with that, and Trey deflated, growling at his friend. "What a fuckin' pair we are."

"At least you have Cass. He's your mate."

That stopped Trey as he went to take a step. "You wanna mate with Rue and this other dude?"

Trey didn't think Kendrick was going to answer. He wouldn't look in Trey's direction as he lifted a tray of clean glasses out of the dishwasher.

"Thinkin' 'bout possibilities," he muttered.

What Trey felt for his friend was mixed. He didn't want him to leave, but he also knew if anyone deserved happiness, it was Kendrick. "Would they be interested?"

He shrugged while emptying the tray of glasses. "Don't know."

"If there's anything I can do to help, ya know I will."

"I know, thanks." He glanced back at Trey. "Did you know ole man Granger? He's selling his small holding out on the Hudson?"

Trey's pulse gave a nice nudge. "I didn't hear that."

"Yep, he's movin' in with his daughter after a fall left him with a dodgy hip. Think it's just gone on the market. You're acquainted with Granger, maybe there's a deal to be struck there. Ya know, if someone was looking to set up a home that had land for their little chick. Also, maybe it's time to get someone to do some of the bar work to free up your time in the evenin's."

"Is that right?"

Kendrick chuckled. "It is. Way I see it, you could take a trip out there and have a look for yourself before it gets busy. And say I put out some feelers to see if anyone is lookin' for some bar work?"

Trey shook his head even as he grinned, his mind racing at all the potentials. "Don't suppose it would hurt."

Chapter Twelve

Cassidy

Cassidy sat on his porch swing, his booted foot rested on the porch railing for leverage as he swung back and forth. This time of the day was his favorite, when he could sit and watch the sun dip behind the rugged mountains, leaving an array of oranges painting the sky and the peaks as the sounds on the ranch serenaded him.

Several of his chicks sat on his lap and Bubba sat on a cushion next to him, lying on his back with his little legs pointed skyward. Luna sat on his rounded belly. The evening was pretty perfect if Cassidy didn't think about what, or rather who, was missing.

He didn't sigh at the misfortune of having a mate who owned a bar, cause it was how they had met. Mated for a whole three weeks and Cassidy already hated the empty feeling that came when he was away from Trey. When he didn't wake up with Trey playing starfish over the top of him, his day didn't start right. Trey's insistence that he not spend his evenings at the bar stung despite the genuine concern he felt coming from Trey for his wellbeing.

This time a sigh escaped, and Lila clucked at him.

He stroked a gentle finger down her back. "I'm fine."

She clucked again and gave him a nip, making him chuckle at how she told him off. "Alright, I'm not. But I can't see no ways to change it."

His gaze strayed back to the sky as he rocked gently, hoping to ease a little of the tension that came from the separation from Trey. In the daytime, when he was working, things weren't as noticeable. The ache was manageable, but when he had nothing else to occupy his time, the loss he felt at not being able to see or touch Trey became a ball of dread in his stomach. It was so bad that he'd gotten sick in the mornings these past few days.

He wanted to shake off the worry that what he was feeling would get worse with each day he kept his thoughts to himself, for fear of chasing off his mate with clingy behavior. It didn't matter he was no longer heading into the bar at night, Cassidy was sleeping for shit and struggled to wake up for work. To find the energy to do what they needed him to do on the ranch. So much so Ethan had taken him aside to have a word about it.

He had said nothing to Trey, but he suspected his mate hadn't missed that there was a problem when he was the one to stop Cassidy coming into the bar at night.

Fuck, he missed him. Seeing him for an hour or two in the day was not the same. The last few days, he'd hardly seen Trey at all.

Is he growing tired of me already?

What nonsense. Are you listening to yourself? Trey is our mate.

Yes, he is, but he's distracted.

He's a busy wolf. That doesn't mean that he's fed up with us. And can I just say this isn't like you.

I don't feel like myself.

It's the pups, that's all.

Cassidy got distracted at the plume of dust coming up the dirt road leading to the cabins when he recognized Trey's truck. His mood instantly improved as he kept swaying, Bubba having squealed when he stopped. "You're spoiled, ya know that?"

Bubba ignored him to settle against his cushion.

His smile was wide and welcoming when Trey came to a stop and got out of his truck, looking sexy in a band T-shirt tucked in his Wranglers. His belt buckle glinted as he strode towards Cassidy, looking like someone who had come with a purpose. An odd tension radiated from him.

Ruffled dark hair framed the attractive face that never failed to make Cassidy's heart skip a beat, but it wasn't the only thing making his pulse increase. Trey ran a shaking hand through his hair.

When his gaze swept over Cassidy, he came up the steps, grinning. "What's this? Ya havin' a party and didn't invite me?"

"I was feelin' lonesome," Cassidy admitted in a moment of weakness. "My girls and Bubba were happy to come keep me company on such a nice night."

Cassidy didn't miss the pause as Trey came to sit on the other side of Bubba, who gave a disgruntled squeal at the disturbed sway of the seat. "I can see that." His gaze when to Lilly and his brows arched. "Is your chick wearin' a knitted top?"

The blush washed over his cheeks as he met Trey's gaze. "My girls like to feel pretty."

They had never talked about his quirks.

"That so?" Trey's grin remained, yet Cassidy witnessed the tension in Trey's stiff upper body.

"It is. I knit." He held Trey's gaze, searching for the look that crossed some folks' faces at his idiosyncrasies. "It's like a hobby. My girls, they like the attention."

Trey chuckled and carefully picked up Lilly and brought her up to his face. Lilly didn't squawk, but she gave Trey a brief peck on his finger. Then she rested her neck on his finger and closed her eyes. "I think she likes me," he murmured, looking so pleased that Cassidy couldn't help but chuckle.

"She does. She can scent that you're mine."

"Good to know."

"What brings you out here? I thought you were workin' late tonight?"

Trey placed his booted foot on the railing and took over rocking. Cassidy sensed Trey was giving himself time to figure out what to say, so he stayed silent. Even though they hadn't spent lots of time together since the mating, Cassidy had watched Trey and figured he knew him better than some. Content just to be close, he went back to watching the sun sink behind the mountains.

"Did you hear ole man Granger is selling his small holding down on the Hudson?"

"Nope." He glanced back at Trey. "I did hear he had a nasty fall and went to stay with his daughter. She buys eggs from the ranch," he said, by way of explaining how he knew.

"He can't manage the fifty or so acres he owns, or the cabin he built for his family some years back. It's a nice place."

Cassidy couldn't quite catch his breath, unsure why he got a case of flutters in his belly. "I'm sure it is. His place is right on the river and the land down there, I hear, is good for rearin' animals."

"Yep. The place could be ideal for someone who might want their own"—he shrugged—"place to raise their chicks."

Cassidy's jaw dropped when what Trey was saying registered. He attempted to speak, coughed, then swallowed hard enough to make his Adam's apple bob madly.

"Chicks?" he squeaked, blushing hard as Trey got up and placed Lilly on the cushion next to Bubba. All his animals were watching Trey as he crouched in front of Cassidy.

"Yep, though you can raise whatever suits. I don't have no preferences." His gaze dropped to Cassidy's middle and several things registered at once, making his mouth water.

Pups.

Pups.

What did you mean by pups?

Really? You couldn't figure out we're pregnant. How?

"I am?" he bellowed, unsettling all the chicks in his lap. They very loudly let him know they weren't happy as they flapped and jumped off him, squawking up at him from both sides. Bubba grunted and snorted, rolling off the cushion, making Luna hop off or get squashed.

"I am?" Trey asked, sounding confused.

And so he should be, when all Cassidy could do was stare at him with everything slotting into place. "Pregnant!" Cassidy exclaimed, uncaring that others were in their cabins and might hear him.

Trey placed a hand on top of his T-shirt and offered him a warm smile. It filled Cassidy up so much he felt he was brimming with... love. "My wolf, he left me know for sure last week—"

"Last week!" Back was the squeak. "Why didn't you say anythin'?"

Trey gave him a pleading look. "I was gonna. Then you didn't mention it, so I thought I'd wait till you were ready. Except I had this idea 'bout doin' this properly."

"Doin' what?" It was Cassidy's turn to be confused. He somehow or other had gotten lost, and he'd be having words with his animal half as soon as he caught his breath!

Trey shifted. One knee went to the porch as he dug a hand into the back pocket of his jeans. "Proposin'."

Cassidy couldn't get his lungs to work. "We're mates," he gasped past the ball of emotion waiting to tumble out of control, along with the tears making his eyes ache.

"Don't mean that I don't wanna marry ya." Trey held a tiny black pouch. "We may have gone 'bout this in reverse. Sex then datin', not that we've done much of that, but I'm hopin' to change that." He tipped the pouch, and a ring tumbled out. Cassidy could see it was not a traditional metal. "When you walked into my bar, you changed me in ways I wasn't expectin'. Changed what I wanted from life. I hired someone to help Kendrick manage the bar, to free up my evenin's. And the last piece, I wanted a place, a home for us. For our family."

Cassidy's breath shuddered out of him at having things he'd never thought possible. Secret wishes he tucked in his heart unfurled in front of him like the gift the wolf on his knee was to him.

"I bought land and a home today, cause I want a life with you. One where we go to bed together and wake every mornin' wrapped in each other's arms."

"More like star fishin' me," Cassidy choked out past the ball of emotions attempting to steal his ability to breathe.

"That too," Trey chuckled. He plucked the ring out of his palm, holding Cassidy's stare. "This is a wolf totem. It's made of several crystals, carved and melded together for a mate's protection. When you wear this, you'll truly be mine in every way."

Cassidy's sniff was undignified, because he had no control over it or the next one as Trey took hold of his hand. The warmth of the skin touching his made it real even before the words.

"Be mine."

There were words inside Cassidy, he knew there were, but he had no clue where and he couldn't get his lips to cooperate. In the end, he gave up and nodded.

"I need words, my little chick."

Cassidy swallowed to wet his mouth, tears streamed down his cheeks. "Yes," he croaked in a hoarse whisper. Then louder, "Yes."

Trey slipped the ring on and it fit perfectly. The weight and feel of it pressing against his skin left Cassidy unable to stop the sob as he heard cabin doors open and the sounds of voices.

Trey rose and scooped him off the seat, seemingly uncaring of the audience they now had. He didn't take his gaze off Cassidy as he called out, "Someone take care of Cass's family for him, we're gonna be busy for a while."

Cassidy buried his face in Trey's neck, overwhelmed, and not from just the proposal, but that Trey would understand that the chicks and Bubba were his family. And that he would make sure someone looked after them.

As Trey carried him into the cabin, Cassidy heard Sunny say, "Don't worry, Cass, I got you covered."

Then, as Trey booted the door shut, he heard Zippy call out, "Where do I find a mate like that?"

"Darling Ranch," someone else replied, laughing, "if you look hard enough."

"No," Cassidy murmured as they stopped in his bedroom, "Ranch-Down is where I found mine."

"Darn straight." Trey's nose rubbed against the side of his neck, down to the claiming bite. "Best thing that bar ever gave me."

Cassidy couldn't argue with that.

Epilogue

Trey

Trey woke with a sharp jab to his ribs. "What," he mumbled, working on figuring what the jab was about.

"The pups," Cassidy gasped in pain. "They're comin'."

Jumping out of bed, Trey kicked the night stand then hopped around in the dark, cursing.

"What you doin'?" Cassidy whined from somewhere on the bed. For the last few weeks of pregnancy, Trey had moved into Cassidy's cabin while they had renovations made to their new home. The bar was too noisy for Cassidy, who had grown sensitive to many things as his pregnancy progressed.

Also, Trey hadn't wanted Cassidy to have to put up with the mess at the new cabin. There was too much dirt and dust created by the carpenter while he added a nursery to the back of the cabin, next to the master bedroom. Cassidy had definite ideas about such things. He wanted their babies close so they would know they were wanted. Trey had no issue with that after Cassidy had opened up about his family, about how they neglected him because he was divergent. Made him share with the chicks in the barn rather than in the house.

Trey did his best not to think about Cassidy's past when his wolf wanted to hunt his family down and tear their heads off. Cassidy being the way he was, he didn't want Trey to do anything. Cassidy just wanted to move forward and create a happy space for their pups. So Trey focused his anger on making that happen.

Toe throbbing, he found the lamp and flicked it on, then wished he hadn't with what he could see happening between Cassidy's legs.

"Oh gods," he exclaimed and, in panic, stepped back, this time hitting his heel on the edge of the door. "Fuckkkk," he ground out, hopping forward. Was this the revenge of the universe for impregnating his mate?

"When you've quite finished," Cassidy said around a low moan, "go call the doc."

Trey swung around and ran out of the room, not noticing he was naked, his feet bare. Down the steps of the porch, he could see the sky was tinging with dawn as he ran towards his truck. He patted his legs, only to groan and curse once more. He ran back into the cabin only to hear mewling coming from the other room, sending him right back into the bedroom.

His wolf went into hiding at the panic coursing through him, which appeared to have stolen the remaining ability to think rationally. He skidded to a halt, his eyes aching with how useless he felt.

Cassidy lifted pain-filled eyes as he faced the end of the bed, rocking on his hands and knees. "Did you... c-call the doc?"

"Fuck," Trey growled and shook himself, going for his phone. "Sorry, I-I... oh gods, you're bleedin'."

"Ring... the fucking... docccccc..." he swayed, his large belly rippling as goo dripped onto the bed from between his spread thighs.

No matter how much they'd talked about this, Trey realized nothing could have prepared him for seeing Cassidy like this. The pain radiated off him and stabbed at Trey's self-control.

"I'm so sorry, I did this to you." Hand shaking, he dialed the doctor, his gaze fixed on Cassidy who grew sweatier by the second. His skin glistened in the light, no part of him still as he rocked.

"Trey... Trey... you there?"

Cassidy's head hung between his shoulders. "Answer him," he snapped breathlessly.

"Sorry Doc. Cass, he's in labor. I don't know what to do," he cried in panic when Cassidy made a sound that sent all the hairs on his body into fight mode. They lifted as his wolf whined in his mind, *Fix this.*

You fucking fix it.

"Keep calm. Soothin' touch, like I showed you. It will help Cassidy deal with the pain. I'll be there as soon as I can."

Trey didn't say goodbye. He threw the phone toward a chair tucked in the corner and climbed back on the bed, avoiding looking at the mess. He ran a hand down Cassidy's back, doing his best not to inhale.

"Tell me what you need," he murmured softly, hoping he didn't sound as frightened as he felt. *Why would anyone want to go through this?*

No matter how many times the doctor had assured him that his little chick's body would adapt to birthing pups, nothing took away the worry. He kept it to himself as Cassidy had grown bigger and struggled to do simple things like bend.

"Not... sure..." he mewled, as his whole body appeared to tighten. "Need to push."

Wasn't this too fast? The doctor had said it would take hours.

Is there something wrong?

His animal sniffed at Cassidy. *No, the pups are fine. They just wanna meet us.*

Well, can you tell them to fucking hold their damn horses as we need the doc?

"Why you stoppin'?" Cassidy demanded in a strangled voice that put Trey on edge.

"Sorry." He went through the moves that the doctor had said would help, keeping all the cursing to himself when it didn't seem to calm Cassidy the way the doctor had assured him it would. The fucker lied to him.

"Go with the feelin'." He hoped that was the right thing to say, because right then, it was all he had.

Cassidy

Waking with an ache in his lower belly, he had thought it was the pups trying to get comfortable, rather than labor. Over the last week, it had gotten decidedly harder to find a position that he liked. He'd lain listening to Trey breathing, using that in an attempt to lull himself back to sleep, only the ache had fast become a pain in his lower back that just didn't seem to have a start, middle or end. It also came with belly cramping.

He had done everything the doctor had said, even stopped sitting on the ground so his girls could acquaint themselves with his belly when he struggled to get up and wrenched his back the week before. The pups weren't due for days, or so the doctor had reassured him after he had gotten the once over after the minor mishap. One he had not told Trey about because his wolf, it turned out, was a worrier. Cassidy was now not doing any ranch work aside from looking after his chicks at Ethan's insistence—or Trey's—after his belly got in the way.

So when it had become impossible to hold still, he had given in and woken Trey. Now he could see his wolf had gone into panic mode again. It helped a little because Cassidy had something else to think about as his mate acted so out of sorts. If he'd had the energy, he would have laughed.

He listened to Trey and decided that going with his feelings was his only option when the pups wanted to meet their parents.

Rocking helped, so Cassidy did that. He mewled and panted because that helped, too. But when that failed, he cried and swore up a blue storm. As voices faded in and out around him, he felt his body prepare.

Sweat dripped from his chin and slid down the sides of his face, making him blink furiously to stop it stinging his eyes. There was the sound of cries, except the pain wasn't stopping, so Cassidy focused and bore down with gritted teeth.

"That's it, my little chick, you're doin' so well, my love."

"Fuck off," he ground out on the next wave of pain. "You're right... this... is all... yourrrrr fault," he growled breathlessly, his body shuddering violently at the next wave of belly clenching pain.

Unsure how long it was before the pain relinquished its hold on him, Cassidy found himself lifted away from the mess and Trey positioned him to rest, his sweaty back against Trey's damp body, their skin sticking together. He panted and sank into the comforting feel of Trey's arms wrapping around him after he tugged up a sheet. Drifting on the exhaustion, his eyes slitted open at the sounds in the room. He could see a huddle of men peeking through the bedroom door. He would let the mortification at being seen like this bother him later, when he got his strength back.

"Have a sip of water for me, my love." A glass touched his lips, and the iciness got him parting them gratefully. He drank deep when the thirst made its presence known.

When the glass moved away, he searched the room, his pulse fluttering madly. "My babies? Where are they?"

Trey kissed the side of his sweaty brow. "The doc is just checking our girls out to make sure they're okay."

"Girls?" he whispered, feeling his world expand with the reality he had daughters.

"Two beautiful baby girls," Trey murmured softly against his skin, a catch in his voice. "They look just like you, Cass."

The doctor walked past the ranch hands, cradling the swaddled girls in the crooks of his arms. Trey was wrong, their beautiful burnt sienna skin was just like their daddies.

"No, they look like us." He held out his arms despite the weakness in them. He didn't worry because Cassidy knew with every fiber in his being that Trey would be there for him, for their girls.

When the doctor carefully placed one girl in each arm, smiling at them, Trey's arms cradled Cassidy and held them all. "I love you."

Cassidy heard chuckles from outside the doorway and ignored them, because hearing his mate say aloud how much he loved him made everything right in Cassidy's world.

"So, what names did you choose for your girls?" This came from the doctor.

Trey's body shook with laughter. "Cass, let his chicks choose."

"Say what?" Ethan muttered as he strode in. "Please tell me you're jokin'?" His face paled as he got a good look at the bed Cassidy remained on.

Cassidy grinned at the room. "I can't, they're my family. They like the letter Z."

There was more laughter. "So, what did they pick?" Ethan asked, sounding resigned and amused at the same time.

Cassidy looked over his shoulder at Trey's amused expression, then down at their daughters. "Say hello to Zuri and Zinnia. The newest members of Darling Ranch."

Thank you for reading!

I hope you enjoyed the launch into the Darling series, in my Divergent Omegaverse world. The first book will be out in late 2025 and I'm working on it with many others in this world. To keep updated, follow me (JP Sayle) on Amazon. Intrigued by the Starling Brothers? Then come meet them in the first three books of the Divergent Omegaverse series on Amazon, the fourth will be out the end of July.

The first book, a prequel, Alpha's Divergent Omega, is free by signing up for my newsletter, which can be done via my website. (Sorry, Amazon doesn't like links for newsletters anymore, but you can easily find me at jpsayle.com)

Taylin's Temptation is the first of the brothers to fall!

Taylin doesn't have a clue how the universe works, but he believes that given the right conditions in which to flourish, love can conquer everything. He is about to put that belief to the test.

Blood of The Damned - Sneaky Peek

Based in the same divergent omegaverse as Starling Enterprises, and based in the town of Bayfield where Darling Ranch is also based, Blood of the Damned – Thorn (a different part of their story which is currently out in Labor of Love anthology is not what we have here. All the proceeds from that anthology go to charity if you want to check it out.) The full book is basically two parts, the small part which is in the aforementioned and will be married with this new part in September, when you'll get all their story! The below is unedited and could change ;)

Chapter One

Ledger

Stunned.

There was no other word for it. Even his cheeky squirrel side was silent in his head. A feat that rarely happened.

The weight of the hand on his lower back guiding him down a busy sidewalk and the sticky mess in his underwear told him that this was no dream. He could feel the warm, soft breeze brushing over his exposed skin. Taste the air and see motes of dust dance in the rays of sunlight. Every sense was hyperacute. The bird cries, the voices of those inside buildings and those on the street, were all now part of his consciousness.

How?

Was it to do with the winged...

He kept pace with the long stride of—whatever he was—the nameless guy unable to make himself stop for a second and consider what the hell had just happened. Ledger wasn't always known for being sensible, he knew this. It was why he'd ended up in Bayfield, but this, for him, was an epic loss of any sensibilities. As in, he had none at all.

Zero.

Zilch.

Nada.

How was he going to explain this to Mr. Vaughn when he'd clearly missed their appointment? It was totally unprofessional on his part to not show up for a meeting. The contract tied him in for a year, this was not a good start despite the fact he'd considered he'd made a wrong decision.

First impressions counted. How did one explain they were having *sex*, being claimed in a back alley instead of taking an important meeting?

And this is what you're thinking about right now?

Yes, yes, it is.

His animal made a noise of disapproval.

We have to pay the bills and—

You're freaking out.

No, I'm not.

Yes, you are.

Ledger shut out his animal side, he wasn't going to think about the other stuff. No, because that would mean having to acknowledge he was freaking out at how he actually encouraged the other man. That wild sex in an alleyway, in broad daylight, with a winged man for anyone to see, was something he'd wanted—*craved*. He'd not only had sex, he had claimed the nameless winged man and felt... he didn't know what he felt, but there was something fundamentally different inside him. It frightened him, even though it was exhilarating.

No, this wasn't exhilarating, it was scary.

It's most definitely exhilarating.

As they stopped silently at the side of a large black SUV, Ledger feigned not to have heard his animal side. Ledger was

more concerned about how easily he acquiesced to getting into the car when he had his own parked on the
opposite side of the street.

Should he just suggest he'd follow behind to wherever
they were going? No, the very idea of leaving, not being
close to the stunner, didn't sit well at all with him. It left
him anxious.

Assisted in the front seat, long tapered fingers buckled
him in, the brush of knuckles over Ledger's lap made
blood flow fast through his veins as he inhaled the rich
scent surrounding him. He avoided looking into the cap-
tivating blue eyes when Ledger heard an indrawn breath
and saw a hint of fang appear.

Was he a vampire bat?

Were they big like that, with huge wings?

Ledger's fingers tingled at the memory of the silky tex-
ture of the feathers as he'd gripped them when...

He pressed a hand to his forehead as the door closed,
and he was alone for a moment. He attempted to pull
himself together. It was pointless as his gaze tracked the
hunk, feeling...

Nothing was in context, nothing, yet it was.

It was madness. He'd had his body snatched and someone had taken over.

Stop being so dramatic.

He resisted telling his squirrel to 'fuck off' when it was
pointless, as he was being dramatic and with damn good
reason.

The moving car brought Ledger's gaze to his...

He pinched his arm hard and squealed at the pain when he couldn't really believe what he was considering had happened.

"What is it, Sweetling?" The hunk of stunningness asked, the smooth voice once more sending delightful sensations to places it had no business going. Not when it made everything even more real.

"I..." he glanced out the window, it was far safer when the urge to climb into the lap of the man—or whatever he was—and get a repeat performance of earlier was out of the question.

Was it?

Yes, it most definitely was. Mortified was what he was when he didn't even know the man's name, and yet he'd let him...

Oh to the heaven's, I'm mated!

I've a mate.

I bit a stranger.

A stranger who is my mate.

It didn't matter which way he looked at it, Ledger had lost his goddamn mind in bumfuck nowhere.

What the fuck was I playing at?

Sweetling, I understand—

Understand, Ledger shouted in alarm at having not considered the man next to him would hear all his thoughts. *We... you... I...*

Ledger twisted in his seat and barely noted the stunning scenery that was so different from the town of Bayfield. Lush hills of green lay spread out before them as the car traveled to where Ledger had not the wherewithal to ask with everything else tumbling around in his head.

He breathed deep, hoping to get his pulse to behave and stop making his ears buzz, only the scent in the confines of the car made his body react and his teeth ache with a desire to... bite.

What is wrong with me?

"There is nothing wrong with you Sweetling, it's the newness of our mating."

He sounded so reasonable.

Only Ledger wasn't feeling reasonable. "I think you should turn the car around." Yes, he needed to regroup, alone. His brain seemed okay with the idea, the center of his chest suggested he was thinking about cutting out his own heart.

He rubbed at the place that ached, disconcerted further when a deep chuckle sent shivers to interesting places as those blue eyes glanced in Ledger's direction. "I have a meeting with my new employer and I'm already terribly late," he tried.

"You're my dhampir, Sweetling."

"Huh?" Ledger figured it was some sort of cosmic joke when he was clueless about the meaning of that word. How could he when he lost his grip on reality?

His sticky, uncomfortable ass said he had. His clothes were a mess. Button's torn of his expensive shirt. Yep, this was not his reality.

"I'll explain everything when we reach the house. I need to concentrate on getting us home safely."

"What?" Ledger felt the squeaky voice was going to become a permanent fixture. "Is there something dangerous on the way?"

Ledger lost his ability to breathe when he became the focus of his mate. The blue of his eyes seemed to glow before the color bled into a fiery red, resembling a ball of a sun about to set. Hunger, it was all he felt between them. A deep-seated craving that felt unnatural with the intensity of it.

"Your eyes… they're red!" he spluttered for something to say to detract from the current need to do some crazy shit. Something else registered, and he blinked slowly when it became apparent they were driving at speed on a twisty road and he was staring at Ledger instead of where the car was climbing up into the mountains. "Watch where we're going." Yep, the squeaky voice was back.

A devilish smile left Ledger aroused and clutching at the front of his trousers. *Talking, an overrated activity, sex that was not!*

He can't drive and have sex with Ledger. It was damn dangerous to even contemplate the insane notion. Thinking like that was hazardous to Ledger's health when suddenly getting naked and biting was all he could think about. It was crazy. It was like he now had a death wish on top of everything else.

Nothing can harm you, Sweetling, now you are bonded to me for eternity.

Smug satisfaction, that's what Ledger felt at that statement, only he wasn't convinced it was his.

He released a shuddery breath when the man next to him returned his gaze to the road.

Ledger became exhausted so suddenly, he felt it start at his feet and rise up making his body feel like a lead weight. He sagged against the seat and shut his heavy-lidded eyes, resting his head back on the headrest.

This was some fucked up shit.

Hurt, a large dose of it got him sighing at realizing he was yet again over sharing his thoughts, not that he had a clue how not to do that. Clueless was what he was.

How did one unravel the mess he'd gotten himself into when he didn't know where to even start with the things his mate said, so why try?

The thought drifted away as the gentle voice of his mate whispered in his mind, *I'll give you all the answers you want. There is nothing to fear. Sleep now, your body is changing.*

His desire to ask what that meant couldn't battle the need for sleep, so Ledger didn't try. He sank into the waiting pool of red darkness, where there was only his mate.

Ledger groggily opened his eyes at the feel of warm air touching his face. Had he fallen asleep? He rubbed at his eyes as his brain came back online and glanced at the open car door directly at his... *mate.*

"Welcome to my home, Sweetling."

The air hissed through Ledger's clenched teeth when his gaze clashed with that of the man now crouching at the side of the door. The desire to jump his bones left him griping the edges of the car seat to prevent himself leaping out. He would not allow himself to be distracted by thoughts of sex. *No.*

No sex.

Talking.

They needed to talk before any nakedness!

"What a pity," his mate murmured.

"What?" Ledger shook his head at how easy it was for his mate to read his thoughts. "No, don't answer that!" He was going to need to watch that, figure out how to keep his thoughts on lock down, until then he'd just have to stop thinking.

How does that work?

He scowled at the stunner and asked, "What's your name?" He needed to get things back onto an even keel... if there was such a position after the last few hours of his life.

The gorgeous mouth formed into a smile that left Ledger struggling not to swallow his own tongue and break the no sex rule right off the bat.

He was pitiful.

"It seems we have done things the wrong way around." He offered his hand. "Thorn Vaughn—"

"Thorn Vaughn, you're shitting me!" Ledger, who had reached for the hand, paused at the thunderbolt hitting him. His eyes widened in disbelief. His mate was none other than Thorn Vaughn... his new boss!

"Oh my! You're Ledger Rain, well, that explains every-thing," Thorn said, making absolutely no sense, looking pleased as punch at the turn of events.

Ledger supposed that was a good thing, but he'd need to think about that after he got his questions answered and found the off switch to sharing. "It explains nothing!" He waved his hand about dramatically. "Nothing makes sense since..." he blushed and the scent of arousal filling his nose—which was not his alone—at where his mind wandered.

Movement behind Thorn brought Ledger's gaze up and he swallowed hard at the sight of the man towering behind Thorn.

As handsome as he was, Ledger got a sense of a wild animal not quite contained in the suit the man wore. The cut was such it fit the broad shoulders and suggested it was handmade for him. The blue of his eyes was much darker than Thorn's, but there was no mistaking the family resemblance.

Thorn rose and turned before the man spoke.

"Are you planning on staying outside all afternoon, because if you are, I'm going to have to kick your ass if I have to talk to that moaning fucker, Amano, again? Four times he's called for you. What happened with..." his gaze flicked to Ledger, and he caught the surprise and a hint of fang. "You bit him!"

Unable to see Thorn's expression didn't stop Ledger feeling the frustration and slight embarrassment at his brother's statement. "This is not a conversation to be had right now."

Shapely brows arched as the man looked between them. "Is that so?" A light of amusement danced in his eyes.

"Brother, seriously."

Ledger felt Thorn's frustration increase before he felt a physical barrier form between him and his mate. It was as if a shutter had come down in his mind when he focused. "Hey, why did you do that?" he questioned aloud, pissed even when he'd wanted to find a way to block his thoughts from Thorn.

Thorn glanced from his brother, the scowl smoothing out. "What Sweetling?"

Ledger felt at a distinct disadvantage, and it increased the pissedoffness he felt. "That mind block thingy you just did. Don't play dumb with me." He got out of the car, needing to at least be able to be standing for this conversation.

"What... oh fuck," came the voice of another man, who looked identical to the one grinning at Thorn.

Thorn's scowl was back. He reached out for Ledger's hand, entwining their fingers together, and a sense of completion came. Much like a jigsaw piece that completed a picture, Ledger might not have all the answers he needed, but this feeling he didn't want to live without.

It scared the fuck out of him.

"Dacian, Calvert, this is Ledger Rain, my dhampir. Sweetling, these are my twin brothers, Dacian and Calvert."

It didn't matter he'd already guessed they were twins, or how proud Thorn was, it was the word dhampir being bandied about like it meant something important that irked him. "There's that word again *dhampir*, does someone want to tell me what the hell it means? In fact, does someone want to tell me what the heck y'all are? Because I don't think you're vampire bats!"

Other books by the author

A Little Christmas Matty Secret

A Little Christmas Terrence

Music & Dreams

A Sucker For Christmas

Sweet Haven

Cruising Right Into Love

A Little Christmas Ollie

Series
Assassins To Order With Lisa Oliver

Marvin – Marvin and Ajani in Audio

Ben – Ben, Teilo & Nico in Audio

Duron – Duron & Beaumont in audio

Conrad – Conrad & Kylo in audio

Dancing With the Devil – Wyatt & James in audio

Tangled Tentacles Series with Lisa Oliver

Alexi #1in audio

Victor #2 in audio

Todd #3 in audio

Markov # 4in audio

Kelvin # 5 in audio

Obsessions Series with Lisa Oliver

Demon's Obsession

Controller's Obsession

Christa's Obsession

Secretary's Obsession

King's Obsession

Little Paws Haven Series
Little Treasure he Hides
Little & Lethal
Enforcers Little Warrior

Divergent Omegaverse Series
Alphas Divergent Omega
Taylin's Temptation
Booker's Bliss
Silas's Sweetheart (preorder out now)

Spin off Series in the Divergent Omegaverse Darling Ranch
Unbar the Barred (this book)

The Potters Creek Series
A Christmas Wish (book one)

The App Series
The App: Daddy kink (book one)
The App: Littles (book two)
The App: Puppy play (book three)

The Flamingo Bar Series

Always More (book one)
The Little Side of Me (book two)
3 Is the Magic Number (book three)

La Trattoria Di Amore Series

Puzzle Pieces (book one)
Dominated but not Subdued (book two)
Made to Submit

The Playroom Series

Mine, Body and Soul: Part One
Mine, Body and Soul: Part Two
Mine, Body and Soul: Part Three
Ferron's Journey: Damaged Part One (book four)
Ferron's Journey: Hidden Part Two (book five)
Ferron's Journey: Revelation Part Three (book six)
Mine, Body and Soul Trilogy
Ferron's Journey Trilogy
Spinoff Love's Heart Print

Dark River Stone Collective Series

The Light Beneath the Dark (Book One)
When Darkness Turns to Light (Book Two)
Running From Darkness (Book Three)

The Billionaire Playground Series

Property of a Billionaire (Book one)
Reluctant Billionaire (Book two)
Billionaire's Muse (Book three)

Heart Stones Series

Blood King

The Manx Cat Guardians Series
Where it all Began: Origins (Book 1)
Seeing Beyond the Scars (Book 2)
Destiny Collides Past and Present (Book 3)
Searching for a Soul to Love (Book 4)
The 12 Disasters of Christmas (Book 5)
Laws of Attraction (Book 6)
The Teacher's Boy (Book 7)
Boxset

Weird & Wacky Shifters
All he wants is a Fingerling
Alphas Fingerling Surprize
A Boy Called Blu

The Rhubarb Effect spin off from Weird & Wacky Shifters
Sticky For You
Rhubarb 2 Go
Ravished By the Rhubarb
Embracing The Stalk
Rhubarb Blush
Stalk of the Town
Rumble of the Crumble

Audio Books

Mine, Body and Soul, Part One: The Playroom Series

Mine, Body and Soul, Part Two: The Playroom Series

Mine, Body and Soul, Part Three: The Playroom Series

Daddy Kink: The App (book one)

Always More: The Flamingo Bar (book one)

When Fake Changed Everything

Ferron's Journey: Damaged Part One

Ferron's Journey: Hidden Part Two

Ferron's Journey: Revelation Part Three

Romance books in a mixed series of M/F and M/M by the Author under a different pen name Jayne Paton

Smith's Corner

Delilah & Dallas (book one)

Layla & Levi (Book two)

Ash & Alora (Book three)

Fox & Faith (book four)

Storm & Stone (book five)

Hunter & Holden (book six)

Crime and Thrillers by the Author under a different pen name J Paton

Headspace

Chozen: Dark MM Crime Drama (Headspace Book 1)

Chozen: Dark MM Crime Drama (Headspace Book 2)

About the Author

Eccentric cake lover who has a passion for words of all kinds. I'm Jayne or JP, I live in the Isle of Man. A tiny place in the Irish sea where all the magic happens. I'm a confessed bookaholic and if I'm not writing I love to snuggle with a book or two...if you catch my drift.

If you're interested in keeping up to date, then I've a few places you can do that, and they're listed below. My website is where you'll find all the different Me's there are, LOL. As I travel this path into the future, I'm going to be writing in different genres so to stop there being any confusion I'll be writing under different pen names.

If you would like to give me any feedback or just have any questions, go ahead and friend me on Facebook, and I would be happy to answer anything. I hope you enjoyed this book and if you would also like to leave a review, then I would love to read your thoughts. Even if you just want to rate it, I'll be grateful

Thank you for being a part of my dream.

Goodreads

Tumblr

Bookbub

Instagram

Facebook

Facebook Author page

JP Manx Minx's